ROYALTY, AMERICAN STYLE

KING OF BASEBALL

LIVIA GRANT

BLACK COLLAR PRESS

Royalty, American Style: King of Baseball

Published by Black Collar Press
Don't miss a release! Sign-up for our newsletter here!

Don't miss a Livia Grant release! Sign up here >>> New Release Newsletter

e-Book ISBN: 978-1-947559-92-9
Print ISBN: 978-1-947559-93-6

BLURB

She refuses to be another notch on the King of Baseball's bedpost.

Playboy Colton King is American royalty... sports royalty that is. The MLB all-star is also the newest millionaire bachelor in an R-rated cable reality show. Six gorgeous women are prepared to do anything to win him as their prize. So why does he only want the one woman on the set he's not supposed to have?

Harper Gardener wasn't supposed to be part of the show, but when Colton turns his charms in her direction, she finds resistance is futile. Can you make it out with her heart still in tact and without being made the fool on national television?

CHAPTER 1

"Colton! Over here! Can I get your autograph?"

Colton King pulled his roller bag through the throng of media crews and diehard fans standing between him and his waiting car. Women's hands groped him. Paparazzi photographed him. Men held out jerseys with the number twenty-one to be signed.

He should be used to the routine, but today, he was done with the attention. His head throbbed, courtesy of the excessive booze he'd consumed the night before. He'd unsuccessfully tried to drown his regret at being conned into participating in one of the stupidest publicity stunts in the history of Major League Baseball. Not exactly the kind of accolade he was going for.

Another damn World Series ring would have been better.

He made a run for it through the final crowd on the sidewalk outside his New York City loft, diving into the back of the waiting limousine. The doorman slammed the door closed behind him, instantly bringing the roar of the crowd to a manageable level.

"Your fans love you. I couldn't be more pleased that you're on board for our little project," Gavin Wallace observed.

"That makes one of us," Colton retorted under his breath.

His friend, and agent, Van Vencinti shot him the evil eye from the seat directly across from him. Considering this stupid stunt was Van's idea, Colt doubled-down.

"Did you bring a copy of the contract? I'd like to review the penalty section again. Just how much will it cost me to abort this nonsense right now?"

He was only half kidding.

He continued before the men could interrupt him. "It's bullshit that you conned me into this during the playoffs. You know damn well I wasn't focusing on the details." He looked his agent in the eye and added pointedly, "You're supposed to be protecting me from doing further damage to my reputation."

Van had been with him from the beginning. He was probably the only person on the planet whom he could count on to give him the unvarnished truth, which made his answer all the more damning.

"This is about more than your reputation. It's about your legacy. You're thirty-six-years- old. You may be the king on the field, but it's time to start thinking about what comes next. You have two... maybe three good years left to tie up the MLB doubles world record, but then what?"

Colt was tired of this conversation already.

"I don't see how this dog and pony show is gonna do squat for my post-career."

"You said you wanted to break into broadcasting."

He scoffed, "And? This is the antithesis of that."

"It's TV. You've got a reputation for being aloof. You may be royalty on the field, and the fans adore you, but you need to work on your insider relationships."

"Last time I checked, it was gonna be six women and me, not baseball or network executives. How the hell will this project move those important relationships forward?" he questioned.

Gavin injected, "Maybe Van didn't mention it, but I don't normally produce reality television for Showtime." He paused, pinning Colt with a glare. "My primary gig is producing athlete interest spots for ESPN."

Ah... now we're talking. Colt glanced at Van who was grinning from ear-to-ear.

"Fine. I guess I'm gonna do this, but why me?"

"Why not you? The name of the show is *Royalty, American Style*. Each season we'll feature a different member of American royalty. Only A-Listers. We already have seasons two and three lined up with a *Grammy Award* winning rock star and a *People's Choice Award* winning movie star. But because ESPN is pulling the strings, we got to choose our leadoff man, and we chose you, the king of baseball. You should be flattered."

More like terrified. "This is just so old. It's been done over and over. I'm a confirmed bachelor. Moreover, I like it that way."

"Why do you think we shopped this to the cable

channels? This isn't going to be *The Bachelor* with chaste kisses and rose ceremonies."

While that assurance relieved him, it equally confused him. "Then I think you'd better explain what it is going to be like, because I haven't got a fucking clue."

Gavin and Van glanced at each other. Colt got the distinct impression they were deciding who got to break the bad news to him.

Van lost. "Think of this as an R-rated *Bachelor*. We've cut the field down to six women. All smoking hot. All with very different attributes they bring to the table. All you need to do is have fun and get to know them. Try them all on for size. Decide if any of them might fit into your future."

"Uh-ha. And when you say R-rated you mean..."

"Your reputation precedes you. You're a playboy. So play. We want edgy. The only rule is nothing non-consensual. The women have all signed NDAs and ironclad contracts. We'll be able to lock anything down from making it on air if we need to. The only thing you can do that will get you in legal trouble is rape. They've signed on for everything else, and since there are cameras in literally every room in the house except the shitter, you don't need to worry about any he said/she said."

"Wait a damn minute. I knew I'd have a crew following me everywhere I went. No one said anything about cameras planted in all the rooms. I expected to have a production schedule. Time off."

"You expected wrong. This is reality TV. There is no script. There will be a filming schedule to support the structure of the show, but for the next six weeks, you're on 24/7."

"Jesus Christ. So let me get this straight. I'm supposed to live with, and sleep with, six women at the same time, all on camera? You're turning me into a porn star. That ought to be a nice transition after baseball. My lifetime .339 batting average will come in really handy... not."

Gavin tried to reassure him. "Settle down. It will be a tasteful show. Of course we won't show everything. Keep in mind, with forty-six cameras running 24/7, we could potentially have thousands of hours of footage. Less than one percent of that will make it into the show. That's why we are taping now, but the debut isn't until January. It'll take that long just to produce the finished product. Just be yourself. Have fun."

He was feeling a bit better until Van added, "And anyway, how is this any different than your normal week? It's not unheard of for you to have six woman going at any given time."

While that may have been technically true a few times when he was younger, Colton felt the need to defend himself. "Listen, the women I date know the score."

"As do the women on the show. Really, this should be business as usual for you," Gavin reiterated.

"Except for the cameras... and that they will be living together and comparing notes... not to mention the fact that I'm supposed to down-select and choose just one of them at the end of the show."

"It'll give you an opportunity to show your acting skills. Who knows? Maybe this could land you a Hollywood contract. You've certainly got the looks and the body for it. You'd bring instant recognition to any project. Look at this as a six-week screen-test."

Colt bit his tongue. What was the point in complaining now, anyway?

The driver weaved them out of the Manhattan traffic and onto the I-95 North, picking up speed as he hurtled Colton towards his doom waiting at the Connecticut mansion. Colt might have tried to look at this as a six-week vacation in the country except for the fact that he now knew it would be more like living under a microscope.

Colton closed his eyes, trying to enjoy his last hour of freedom from prying eyes, but he had to endure listening to the other men in the car plotting his demise. He replayed the last two days in his head, details finally falling into place. The show had sent a camera crew to Manhattan to interview him for the first episode and promo shots. It had been fun to show off the luxurious loft he'd worked hard to make his own. They'd followed him as he'd received the VIP treatment out on the town; dining in a five-star restaurant; dancing in an exclusive club; drinking top-shelf liquor. Shit. And getting a blowjob from that groupie under the table. He sure as hell hoped they hadn't filmed that.

He must have dozed off, because when he jarred awake, they were off the highway, weaving through thick woods surrounding curved roads. Despite the trees being bare in the November chill, he could see the serene beauty of the rural setting, bringing back memories of his childhood. The only signs of life were gated entries every half-mile or so, the driveways they protected so long that no houses were visible from the road.

At the top of a hill, the driver slowed, stopping at the electronic keypad stand next to a twelve-foot wrought-iron fence. The opening of the gate coincided with a lurch of Colt's stomach. His light lunch was threatening to reappear.

Unaware of his passenger's discomfort, the driver wound them around a curve that opened up to a long, tree-lined driveway. To the left was a well-manicured lawn with what looked like several seating areas centered around fountains and monuments, giving it the feel of a secluded park in the city.

But it was the right side of the lane that held his attention. A white fence enclosed a meadow where over a dozen magnificent horses grazed, several looking up from their meal as they passed.

"We lucked out getting this place. It's been on the market for almost a year. The owner passed away and the executor of the estate is holding out for big bucks. The good news is that it was still furnished and available for us to rent. They had retained the caretakers to maintain the stable and the property. All we needed to do was supplement with our support personnel. There are nine bedrooms, twelve bathrooms, a movie theater, gym, pool... you name it. Think of it as a vacation."

"A vacation where every word I say and every action I take is being recorded."

"And how is that different from your normal day? You're in the spotlight every time you leave your house."

"Precisely. But you're telling me this is my house for the next six weeks. You see my dilemma."

"You're worrying over nothing. This is right up your alley."

The car had stopped. The driver was holding open the door. Colton stepped out to what felt like his doom.

COLTON TOOK one last look at his reflection in the full-length mirror, liking what he saw. The producers had filled his temporary closet with a wide array of designer clothes, most custom-made specifically for him by his personal tailor in the city. One of three expensive watches from the dresser complemented his black suit. He'd asked the hair and makeup guru to leave a day's scruff on his chin to remind the ladies he was about to meet he wasn't all polished and clean like his appearance might lead them to believe.

He'd had enough time to think through his game plan. Gavin and Van had led him on a tour of the property, helping him devise a plan to divide and conquer the contestants of the show. And that is what he'd think of them as—contestants on a game show. It may be a fucked-up kinda game, but it was one he knew well.

He wound his way through the opulent home, too distracted to stop and look at the ornate workmanship of the wood trim or the richness of the carpets and decor. He needed to stay on point, focus on making a good impression, not only on the six women he was about to meet, but on the support staff as well since he was intimately aware that they would be deciding what snippets of his life over the next six weeks made it on screen and which would fall to the cutting room floor.

The show's narrator and host, Ryan Remmings, waited for him at the bottom of the steps of the grand foyer. As Colton made his way down the curved staircase, he allowed himself to get a bit excited at the thought of watching six beautiful women take the same path. As much as his head lamented his rash decision to participate in the show, he was equally confident his cock was going to enjoy the challenge immensely.

"Colton, perfect timing." Ryan reached to shake his hand. Colt tried to ignore the movement of the cameraman off to his right who was trying to get the shot and yet stay out of the action. The host must have noticed. "Just try to ignore the cameras. After a few days, you won't even notice they're there."

He seriously doubted that.

Ryan went on, unaware Colt was only half paying attention. A heavenly aroma wafted to him, smelling very much like his favorite dish from his favorite restaurant. It distracted him just long enough that he almost missed Ryan's invitation to look up the stairs.

Colt turned back towards where he'd come just in time see a drop-dead gorgeous woman waiting at the top stairs, holding there until their eyes met, ensuring she had his full attention before beginning her descent.

When her high-heels hit the marble floor, he noticed she stood at his height. Tall and lean, the brunette with long, thick hair and olive skin looked like she should be on a runway.

Ryan made the introductions. "Colton, I'd like to introduce you to your first lady, Cleo Tavares. Cleo, this is Colt King. Among other things, Cleo was born and raised in Brazil. She was the runner-up in the Ms. Universe pageant three years ago and has since been working full-time as a runway model in Paris, New York, and Milan."

Okay, so maybe this wasn't going to be such a bad deal after all. He reached out to take her hand, bringing it to his lips in a show of chivalry. "Nice to meet you, Cleo."

"Very nice to meet you as well." Her accent was thick, but sexy as hell.

"Where do you call home these days?" His charm had flown out the window, surprisingly intimidated by the Amazon beauty.

Stay calm. She's just another target.

"I prefer to stay in New York City, but unfortunately, I have had some pesky visa issues. Luckily, the show was able to influence immigration to allow me to stay."

So... Colton read that as a good sign. She was play-date material, but would be out of his hair once deported. Then he wondered if she were participating to try to catch herself a rich American husband.

Well, fuck that shit.

Thankfully, Ryan wanted to keep things moving along, inviting her to proceed into the next room where the long dining room table would host their nightly dinners together.

"Ready to meet our second lady?" Ryan asked, but he didn't bother waiting for Colt's reply, turning instead to the staircase to nod at the blonde at the top of the stairs.

She looked familiar, but Colt couldn't place her by the time she stepped on the foyer marble. She'd chosen a sporty outfit with a frilly mini-skirt, and the scooped neckline of her blouse showcased her ample breasts. The spray-on tan looked fake, but the defined muscles of her arms and legs were the real deal. This chick worked out.

"Colton, this is Kylie Kelly. You might recognize her. She's the queen of the tennis world these days, much as you are the king of baseball. We thought you two might enjoy a chance at hitting it off."

As soon as Ryan mentioned her name, things clicked into place. Colt followed Kylie's Instagram and Twitter accounts where she regularly pulled thousands of hits within minutes of her postings. Not only an athlete, she was a walking marketing machine. This was potentially something his reputation could benefit from, if it went well—or something that could bring him down, painting him as the bad boy, if it didn't. Just what he needed, to get thousands of Kylie fans hating him.

The third woman to stand at the top of the staircase was as different from the first two as possible. Dressed in a floral sundress, despite the November weather, the strawberry-blonde moved cautiously down the steps—less sophisticated, but just as lovely. Her eyes focused more on her feet than on the bachelor waiting for her, and when she reached the foyer and looked up at him, her pale green eyes widened, complementing the smattering of freckles across the bridge of her nose.

"Colton, I'd like you to meet Sophia Steward. We found her through one of the contests we setup around the country. She was chosen by our producers out of the four-thousand women who sent in videos to compete to be here. She's from Iowa City."

"Hi, Sophia." He leaned in for a quick hug, noting how she felt as stiff as a board.

Her simple, "Hello," was lovely. Unlike the first two women, Sophia felt more like the girl next door. Not exactly the kind of woman he spent a lot of time with these days, but honestly, she seemed to be a lower risk of blowing up in his face when things went bad.

By the time the fourth woman stood at the top of the staircase, Colton had started to put together exactly how much trouble he was in. These women were all drop-dead gorgeous and seemed to be lovely on the inside as well. How the hell was he supposed to portray his playboy routine with all of them living under the same roof? He said a small prayer that the remaining women turned him off, in hopes of narrowing the field early on.

It wasn't meant to be. Contestant number four was Aviana Perry, a high-powered tax-attorney from Manhattan. Her tailored business suit was cut short to showcase her long legs. She could have been a model, like Cleo, had she chosen that path, but when she opened her mouth, he knew she was as intelligent as she was beautiful. He looked to his left at his friend Van who was hanging out behind the cameraman. His agent gloated, knowing Colton's weakness for intelligent women.

Sure the remaining women could not possibly surpass the first four, Colton was at first relieved to see contestant number five walking down the stairs. While there was nothing wrong with the young woman, there was equally nothing spectacular that stood out either. In fact, he glanced at Ryan, confused as the woman closed the final feet between them before launching herself into his arms, hugging him so hard that she actually lifted her feet off the ground, wrapping her legs around his waist and squeezing as if they were about to do the down and dirty then and there had they not been fully dressed and surrounded by a dozen people.

Colt chuckled as Ryan explained. "This is Lucy Scott. She won her spot on the show by competing against hundreds of other Colton King enthusiasts. She describes herself as your number one fan, heading up the Austin, Texas, chapter of your fan club." Ryan tried to help Colt peel her out of his arms, but it got harder when the men realized she was sobbing against his shoulder.

"I can't believe I finally get to meet you," she cried. "I swore I wasn't going to make a fool of myself, but here I am crying like an idiot."

Colt would have pegged her as a Texan just from her accent. Like a gentleman, he pulled the handkerchief from his inside pocket, handing it to her to dab at her eyes and blow her nose.

"It's nice to meet you, Lucy."

"Oh. My. God. You said my name!"

Ryan looked alarmed. "Lucy, we talked about this. You're going to be spending six weeks here with Colton. You don't need to act like he's never going to speak to you."

"I know. I know. I'll pull it together. It's just so exciting. You can ask me anything. Go ahead. I have all of your stats memorized." When Colt didn't speak, she prodded him again. "Go ahead! Ask!"

Well, okay then. "So, Lucy, what is the total number of double-base hits I've racked up in my major league career?"

"That's too easy! You ended the season at 699, in fifth place for the all-time record. You only have twenty-five to go to tie Ty Cobbs for fourth, and ninety-four to take over the number one slot. If you hit thirty-one each of the next three seasons, you'll take the record, which should be easy for you because you..."

Ryan had to hold his hand up to get her to stop talking. The moderator tried to laugh it off, but Colt could see exasperation in his expression. "As you can see, you have a super-fan. There were few others in the competition who were as big of baseball fans as Lucy here."

"I don't doubt it."

He already knew he'd need to keep his distance from this one. She was too impressionable, and a little attention would go a long way.

"And finally, last, but certainly not least, we have Maya Romanovski joining us all the way from Moscow. Maya is a dancer."

Something in the way Ryan said the word dancer made Colt glance his way. The men shared a knowing glare just before he looked up to see a woman who could easily be mistaken for a hooker in the outfit she was wearing. Skirt cut up to her ass, top cut down to her tits and the part in the middle poured into the skin-tight spandex strips that exposed her pierced bellybutton. She swayed her way down the steps slowly in her platform heels, rocking her hips to unheard music while undressing Colton with her eyes. Her makeup was heavy, and his twisted mind couldn't help but picturing her falling to her knees on the marble floor to suck him off as her salutation. The deep red of her lipstick would make a nice souvenir on his groin because sure as shit, he knew she could deep-throat any cock pointed her way.

Speaking of cocks, his was currently doing a nice rendition of a salute, which was only made worse when Maya leaned into a full-body hug, daring to grab his package and squeeze it through his pressed trousers.

"I see you are glad to see me too, sweetheart," she said slyly.

Colt cleared his throat, trying to extricate himself from her wandering hands, knowing that the cameramen were setup at the perfect angle to capture every sordid detail of her greeting.

"Nice to meet you, Maya," he added lamely, trying to focus on calming his erection down before she pulled away.

That effort was made impossible when she leaned up to whisper in his ear loud enough for everyone within ten feet to hear her. "My room is the farthest down the hall. I requested it so we wouldn't keep the others awake all night when you visit me."

Colton couldn't help it. He burst out laughing. The whole scene was so ridiculous that it was funny. The smooth narrator, Ryan, was left speechless as Colton played it up, stealing his first kiss for the camera from the sexual animal in front of him. While she wasn't really his type, the one thing Maya had going for her was he knew he wouldn't be hurting her feelings when he ditched her at the end of the game. The other five women, he couldn't say the same.

As she sashayed away to join the others, Colton whispered, "I'm guessing you guys stocked up on condoms?"

Ryan slapped him on the back, finally snapping out of his trance. "Oh, never fear. We've stocked up on lots of things."

Colton didn't know exactly what that meant, but he suspected he might have some fun finding out.

CHAPTER 2

Harper Gardener rushed around the kitchen island, rescuing the homemade Italian bread from the oven just in time to avoid it being burned. Not for the first time that day, she berated herself for not driving up from the city the day before so she could familiarize herself with the restaurant-style kitchen she'd call home for the next six weeks.

She knew how lucky she was to land this job. If she hadn't, she'd probably be squatting on her best friend Vivian's couch on the lower-east side, or in her run-down Honda on her way home to Illinois with her tail between her legs. This job may be a temporary stay of execution, but she knew there was a very good possibility she'd be packing-in her dream of making it in NYC and heading home before Christmas.

"Okay, introductions are finished. The participants have mingled over drinks for thirty minutes. Mr. Wallace gave the green light for me to start serving the first course as soon as they're seated," Cecelia, long time caretaker of the property, confirmed.

"Sounds good. The salads are in the walk-in fridge on a tray to the right. I made a couple homemade dressings, too."

"Wow, such talent. You've only been here a few hours." The kind, older woman's smile was genuine, a rare commodity in Harper's life recently. "It's so nice to have the kitchen back in use again after all these years. The Ungers weren't well the last few years they resided here, and well, the main house has been empty now going on a year."

"I can't believe this dream kitchen has been going to waste. And don't tell Mr. Wallace, but I cheated a bit. I made one of my signature dishes from my old job. I could make this ravioli dish in my sleep. I'll have to work my way up to harder entrees after I get the lay of the kitchen," Harper added.

But it wasn't the kitchen she was worried about. It was the long list of special requests from the temperamental participants in the show that concerned her. Having dietary restrictions was one thing. The lists of things some of these women refused to eat read like a culinary final exam: what meal can you make from water and this stalk of celery?

Two identified as vegan, which in and of itself was difficult for a chef responsible for feeding a large group of people. Another refused to eat carbs or dairy. A fourth hated vegetables and seafood, while a fifth would only eat vegetables and seafood. Add in a gluten-free and sugar-free request, and she felt like the producers should call her part of the show *Mission Impossible*.

This should be fun.

The one thing she knew for sure was that they would all be hating tonight's dinner. She'd kept it simple, with soup, salad, pasta, and dessert, and based on the information sheets, each of the women would be equally disappointed by their first meal in their temporary home. She could only hope they'd be too distracted by the misogynistic asshole they were all trying to woo to notice.

Harper had taken a few minutes of her break to do a Google search on Colton King and had immediately wished she hadn't. His clear baseball prowess aside, the guy was nothing short of a man-whore. Rarely photographed with the same woman more than once, he'd managed to live thirty-six years as a confirmed playboy. King of baseball, indeed. More like king of one-night stands. She could only hope the jerk stayed out of her kitchen, because she wasn't sure she'd be able to keep her opinion of his treatment of women to herself.

Cecelia had returned, a frown on her face.

"Is everything okay?" Harper asked.

"Those are some sour women. We're only on day one, and already they're complaining about this or that. I don't envy your job trying to make all of them happy, Ms. Gardener."

"Please, call me Harper. I didn't have enough time to deal with their special requests tonight. I'll have to study the demands and go shopping tomorrow with a new plan."

Cecelia smiled. "You sure made Mr. King happy, though, when I told him we were having mushroom ravioli for the main course. He told me it was his favorite entree at this restaurant he likes to go to in the Italian Village. I told him that was a coincidence. Didn't you say you used to work at an Italian restaurant in the city? Wouldn't that be something if he was talking about your ravioli?"

"Yeah, something," she said, non-impressed. Every Italian chef worth their salt could make this dish.

Members of the filming crew took turns flitting through the kitchen, introducing themselves and grabbing a bite to eat when they could. Everyone was very nice, other than the complaints she could hear through the swinging door separating the kitchen from the formal dining room. Comments like, "It's a good thing I brought a bag of my own food" and "I'm not going to gain ten pounds while I'm here," got Harper's blood simmering. She was relieved when the meal was over, and the participants all left to go get to know each other in some other area of the big house.

"Excellent meal, Ms. Gardener."

Harper turned to find the producer of the show in the doorway. "Thanks, but I don't think your dinner companions agreed."

"You made Mr. King happy, and you gave him and the future audience a good chance to see how the contestants handle adversity."

She chuckled. "Adversity? I asked them to eat carbs."

"Precisely. Keep up the good work. I'm glad I took Georgio's recommendation to hire you."

Her heart stopped. "What do you mean his recommendation? I applied for the position on my own."

The producer looked like he'd said too much, but she pressed him until he added, "How do you think you got the notification of the opportunity?"

"That sonofabitch." She threw the hand towel down she'd been drying dishes with and started pacing, putting together the puzzle pieces. She'd known the asshole was cheating on her. She'd confronted him, and he'd lied. She'd threatened to leave, for Vivian's couch, but then this amazing opportunity had fallen into her lap at the last second. She'd thought it was divine fate, when in reality, it had been her no-good ex-boyfriend ensuring she'd move out, so he could carry on his affair with the maître d' of his restaurant.

"I'm sorry. I thought you knew."

"Oh, I think I did. It helps to know the score."

"Well, regardless, keep up the good work. I'll see you at seven for breakfast."

IT WAS late by the time Harper turned off the last light in the kitchen and left through the back door to make the short walk to the pool house. She'd been relieved to find they didn't have enough bedrooms in the main house for her. She preferred to stay hidden away from the residents when she wasn't working.

She tried not to think about the contract she'd signed agreeing to be on camera 24/7. It wasn't like she'd ever have a camera crew assigned to her for the reality show, but just being in the big house, she was constantly aware of the cameras hidden away where it was too easy to forget they were there. She longed to be in her own room where she could finally relax, if only for a little bit.

She'd arrived late and hadn't been able to unpack. She had two bags that she'd need from her trunk. Feeling tired, she almost let it wait until the next day, but knew she'd need her toiletry bag with her toothbrush and contact lens solution.

As she began walking across the yard, the whinny of horses could be heard from the well-lit stable, drawing Harper in. She'd grown up on a farm. As a kid, horses had played an important role in her life, but choosing to go to culinary school in downtown Chicago had taken her away from home, and she'd only been back for short visits since.

Cecelia's husband, Charlie, was brushing down a lathered horse when she approached the first stall.

"He's beautiful," she observed.

"Why, you scared me, Ms. Gardener. I'm afraid the Mrs. and I are not used to having folks around. It's gonna take some getting used to having you here."

"I'm sorry if I frightened you. I just saw the light on, and well... I love horses and wanted to check it out."

"Do you ride?" he inquired.

"I used to. It's been a while."

"It's a bit like riding a bike. I'm sure you'll remember."

"Oh, I wouldn't impose."

"No imposition at all. In fact, over half of the horses we stable are for city folks too busy to get out here to ride very often. They pay us to not only feed and care for their animals, but to make sure they get regular exercise. If you'd like to ride, just say the word, and I'll hook you up with Dolly down at the end of the paddock. She's a good mare for you to get reacquainted with riding again."

His offer was most unexpected. "That would be amazing. I never dreamed I'd get to ride out here. I'll be a bit busy for a few days, but maybe over the weekend."

She patted the soft nose of the gelding he was brushing, drawing a whinny from the handsome sorrel.

"Sounds good. Confirm with Cecilia, and I'll have a saddle and bridle waiting for you."

Harper reluctantly said goodnight, knowing she had a lot of work ahead of her before she could call it a night. Cecelia had told her they'd moved her car to the ten-car climate-controlled garage. Her Honda would be spoiled when it was time to return to city street parking in December.

It was eerily quiet as she approached the garage. Gone were the city cars and buses, honking cab drivers and crazy people talking to themselves. Out here, those sounds were replaced with frogs croaking and an occasional hoot owl in the distance.

She stopped to admire the scenery, taking in a deep breath of clean air. The moon was half full, shining just enough light on the land to highlight the property's pond and a small lake in the distance.

"Nice night for a walk." The masculine voice in the shadows scared the bejesus out of her.

"Who's there? Mr. Wallace, is that you?" Harper swung in the direction of the voice, only able to make out the tall frame of a man in the darkness, leaning against the trunk of just one of the many mature oak trees on the grounds. Her heart leapt in her throat realizing how secluded the property was, not sure if Mr. Finnegan would hear her from the stables if she cried for help.

Her pulse spiked up a notch when Colton King stepped out from the shadows, his hands raised above his head as if to surrender, a broad grin visible in the moonlight. The glow of the cigar in his left hand gave her the answer as to what he'd been doing sneaking around outside.

"Oh for crap's sake, you scared me. Don't sneak up on a girl like that," she huffed, both relieved and aggravated at his presence. She'd never been afraid of the dark before, and it pissed her off that she was reassured to have company as she was about to go into the dark outbuilding. She made a mental note to grab the flashlight from her glove box to carry in her coat pocket for the future.

Harper pushed past the baseball player, refusing to return the smile still playing at his lips in the dim lighting. She opened the side door to the garage and felt around the wall, looking for the light switch.

"Here. Let me get my cell phone out." Colton King had followed her into the darkened building and was helping to search for the switch. Their fingers brushed briefly in the dark and she quickly pulled her hand back, not wanting anything to do with the guy who smelled like clean soap and cigars.

The flashlight on his phone almost blinded her when he switched it on pointed right at her. "Oh, sorry about that," he apologized, but the smile on his face didn't make him look very sorry.

She frowned.

"What? Did I do something to offend you?"

She ignored his question, determined to keep her distance from lover boy. Harper reached past him to flip on the now visible switches, blanketing the garage in florescent lighting.

"Whoa," they said in unison as they turned their attention to the contents of the garage. Harper was no expert on luxury cars, but even she knew there was a fortune's worth of vehicles parked side by side in a neat row.

Colt started walking the line, naming the cars as he went. "I'm not good on guessing years, but this is a vintage Jaguar convertible. A Corvette from the 70s. A Maserati. A Lamborghini. A Land Rover. A Bentley. An Audi. And..." He stopped, looking back confused. "One of these things just doesn't belong here."

What a joker. Did he really just quote *Sesame Street*?

"That's my car, you big jerk," she huffed at his deserved insult.

"Listen, lady, I don't know who the hell you are, but I'll ask again. Have I done something to offend you?"

She sailed past him, anxious to get her bags and hide in her room. "It doesn't matter who I am. Thanks for the help with the light." She hoped her brisk comment would send him on his way.

She wasn't so lucky. She'd just gotten to her car when she felt his hands on her arms, spinning her around until her back was jammed against the window. He crowded her, stopping shy of actually touching her. He was luckily a good six inches taller than her, giving her the perfect excuse to stare at his chiseled chin instead of into his eyes as she tried to defuse the situation.

"Listen, I'm just tired, okay? I drove out from the city, had to work all day and now I need to get my stuff upstairs and unpacked, so I can plan out everything for tomorrow." She stopped short of apologizing because—well—she wasn't sorry.

Was it her imagination or was he leaning closer? She jumped when his index finger lightly touched her chin, lifting her face until she had no choice but to acknowledge him.

Her breath caught. He was more handsome in person than in any of the thousands of pictures on the Internet. For the first time, she had an inkling of why so many otherwise intelligent women might lower themselves to be used by the guy and then thrown away.

It was a good thing she was stronger than that.

"I'm Colt."

"Duh."

That made him smile which only made him more good-looking... virile... suave...

She shook her head as if to clear the unwanted thoughts with a reboot.

"Now. Let's start again. I'm Colton King, and you are?" His question hung in the air.

Oh for crying out loud, they'd be here together for six weeks. There was no way he wouldn't figure out who she was. "I'm Harper Gardener. I'm the chef they hired to cook for the cast and crew for the next six weeks."

It was a good thing her car was propping her up, because the hug he scooped her into had a way of making her knees weak.

"That was the best damn mushroom ravioli I've had. It was even better than Georgio's in the Italian Village."

Holy shit. What were the odds?

"Actually, I would argue that it was exactly like the dish from Georgio's."

"You've eaten there?"

"No, I got fired from there. It was my dish."

"What? I won't be able to get it any more when I'm in town?"

So typical, looking out for himself. "I'm so sorry my career's demise will be an inconvenience for you."

"Okay, I guess I deserved that one. Why the hell would you get fired? You have skills."

"Apparently not the right ones." When he waited expectantly for clarification on her cryptic answer, tears crept into her eyes as she added vulnerably, "George and I worked together... lived together. I thought we might even get married one day, but that was before he decided to dip his nib in the new girl. Suddenly, I'm out of a job. An apartment. So yeah, I'm a little angry at men in general right now."

"What a fucking asshole."

The vehemence of his anger surprised her.

"Isn't that a little hypocritical of you? I mean, don't look now, but you're going to be sleeping with six women for the next six weeks, not to mention the hundreds, if not thousands, in your notorious portfolio. I'm pretty sure there might be a few hundred women out there feeling exactly like I do right now, only with your picture pinned to the voodoo doll instead of George's."

Colt fell forward, trapping her body between his and the car door, anger flaring in his eyes. "First, I've barely even met the women in the main house, let alone slept with them. And while, yes, I may have played the field over the years, I sleep like a baby at night knowing I have never—not once—cheated on a woman I was in a monogamous relationship with. I've been nothing but honest with the people I go out with. That may seem like splitting hairs to someone not involved, but any woman who complains I cheated, wasn't paying attention."

Harper was stunned into silence. He was close enough she felt his breath on her cheek as he fought to calm his burst of anger. Her misguided read of George aside, she thought of herself as a good judge of character. In that moment, she knew Colt King was telling the truth.

"I'm sorry. It's really none of my business anyway."

He hesitated, pressing against her long enough that, even through her coat, she could feel the hardness of his athletic body. She needed to put some distance between them.

Her hand snaked between their bodies to press against his immobile chest. Seconds later, he stepped back, this time shaking his head as if to shake an unwanted thought out. She used the opening to dash towards the back of her car, popping the trunk with her key fob. She wrestled her biggest suitcase out before reaching back in for her smaller carryon bag. When she turned back, Colt had the handle raised and was pulling the bag away, between the cars and towards the exit.

"You don't have to do that!" she called out to him. "I can handle it."

He waited for her at the door, slapping her hand away when she went to grab her bag. "You're really a stubborn woman; you know that?" He flipped off the lights, blanketing them in darkness before ushering her out into the yard. She was about to reach for the bag again, when he picked up the heavy case. "There's no way you can roll it across the yard on these stones. Stop being a baby, and let me help you. Where is your room?"

There was no way in hell Colton King was going to help her to her room. Awareness hit her, and she swung around in a circle, frantically looking for a hidden camera crew.

"Don't worry. I ditched 'em already. I'm guessing they'll figure out my tricks eventually, but for tonight at least, I'm sans cameras." Her face must have registered her relief, but he added a jovial, "That's exactly how I feel too."

Recognizing he was being genuinely helpful, she started walking back towards the pool house. She could hear his shoes crunching on the stones behind her. She'd dropped her briefcase and purse in her apartment earlier, so she at least knew where the light switch was to illuminate the first floor of the impressive space.

Colton's impressed whistle made her smile. She'd have thought a guy like him was used to this kind of almost gross opulence. The space was the size of a basketball court, two stories high, with walls of windows from floor to ceiling. She hadn't explored, but she could see a whirlpool, heated pool, lap pool, and billiards area from the entrance.

"The caretakers, Charlie and Cecelia, told me there's a gym, kitchen, stocked bar, and locker rooms behind the wall at the other end."

"Impressive."

"If you say so. I say, excessive."

He pinned her with a stare she didn't know how to interpret. She had to force herself to look away, moving towards the flight of stairs to her right that led to the apartment above. "My place is up here. If you want to leave the bag there, I'll come back down for it."

"Do you ever just let someone help you and then say thank you?"

His question annoyed her. She wanted to keep him at arm's length, and it was getting harder and harder the nicer he acted.

"I'm independent; is that a crime?"

"Crime? No. A shame? Yes."

"Why do you care so much?"

They were at her door. Not wanting to invite him in, she turned, pressing her back against the hard wood as he crowded closer, just as he had in the garage. The guy had some serious personal space issues.

"I guess because every single other person on the property wants something from me. It's refreshing to find someone who doesn't."

"And yet you helped me anyway." She softened. "Thank you."

For the briefest of moments, she wondered if he

would kiss her. He stepped back, taking a deep breath of his own before adding a quiet, "Goodnight, Harper Gardener."

He'd turned and was halfway down the stairs when she caught her breath again. Only after the bang of the door to the outside confirmed she was alone, did she whisper, "Goodnight, Colton King."

CHAPTER 3

The morning sun was just peeking over the horizon to the east as Colt made his way across the open drive towards the pool house. He'd been having increasing trouble sleeping in the two weeks since his arrival in Connecticut. The stress of balancing six competitive women, one demanding producer, and a bossy agent was aggravating enough. But if he was honest with himself, it was the internal reflection he'd been forced to go through in the process of filming that weighed on his mind when he closed his eyes. He missed his hectic game schedule that kept him too busy to think overly hard about anything except baseball.

But faced with the daily questions of what he planned to do with the rest of his life, both professionally and personally, he'd fallen into a rare funk, which was not exactly conducive to building a compelling reality TV show, unless they wanted to change the focus from his love life to his mental health.

Colt let himself into the quiet building, glad to see he

had the space to himself. Like his previous trips to the gym or sauna, his eyes fell on the stairs to the apartment above, thinking of the chef who was sleeping there. He'd only been able to talk with Harper a few times since that first night, and it had always been in the main house with cameras and people all around. She'd been aloof, unwilling to find herself alone with him. Yet, it had made him happy to catch her sneaking glances his way when she thought he wasn't looking. She blushed beautifully when he winked at her.

He'd be lying to himself if he didn't admit to being disappointed she wasn't walking down the steps even now. She was an anomaly. A unique mix of funny, intelligent, and beautiful. He may not know why yet, but she'd captured his attention in a way few had in the past.

Making his way to the glass table next to the lap pool, he threw his phone, keys, and towel down before stripping off his workout clothes to reveal his speedo. Grabbing his goggles, he headed to the starting block at the far end of the pool.

The water was cool as he dove in, jolting him awake as he sluiced through the wetness, enjoying the stretch of his muscles. He wasn't a particularly strong swimmer, but he loved the workout water resistance provided his body.

And boy did he need it.

His thoughts returned to the woman upstairs, remembering the amazing dishes she'd been surprising him with each day. If he wasn't careful, he was going to pack on poundage before taping ended.

Twenty laps later, Colt dragged his fit body out of the pool, grabbing his towel and phone and beelining it to the heated whirlpool. He sunk his body into the warmth, letting the pounding jets beat away at his muscles, helping him relax. Knowing time was getting short before his assigned camera crew would seek him out, Colt grabbed his phone and dialed Van.

"Do you know what time it is?" his friend grumbled.

"As a matter of fact, I do. I've already got twenty laps in. How about you?"

"I was going to sleep in today. My first meeting isn't until ten."

"Screw that. I need your help. This whole thing is a big mistake. You have to get me out of here."

"Hey, hold on. I thought things were going great. Gavin is happy."

"And I'm miserable, and might I remind you, you work for me."

"Let's slow down. What's going on?"

"What's not? Five of the six women are cutthroat, coming at me like I'm a piece of steak, except they're all fucking vegans so I guess that's a bad analogy."

"Okay, that's kinda bad. But how about the sixth one? Have you connected with her? Maybe she's the one?"

"Sophia? God, no. She's so quiet and timid, she barely let's me hold her chair for her at dinner. Even if I wanted to be with her, I'd bet my life she's frigid."

"Well, you should at least be getting some good ass from the others."

"Knock it off, will you? I'm the first to admit I've played the field loose over the years, but never like this. Not pitting women living under the same roof against each other. And never with women I didn't choose myself."

"Is that what this is all about? Gavin chose them for you?"

"No, dammit. I just don't know what the hell I'm doing here and how you think this fiasco is going to do my career any good. Let's just assume I even wanted to sleep with these women. If I play the playboy, I come off looking like a fucking asshole. If I don't, Gavin and Ryan get all over me for acting too honorable. Can you believe that shit? They actually called me a choir boy!"

"There has to be some mistake. No one could ever confuse you with a choir boy. You sing like shit."

"Fuck you. I called you for some real advice, not for you to gang up on me too."

"Okay, okay. I'm sorry, but you have me a bit confused here. Since when is being faced with having sex with beautiful women a bad thing for you?"

That was just it. Right there. The million-dollar question.

"I can't explain it. It just feels... slimy. Maya snuck into my room and woke me up with my dick in the back of her throat yesterday."

"That doesn't sound like a real problem, buddy."

What was wrong with him? It had felt fucking fantastic at the time. That woman's mouth had skills. But it had been later that it had bothered him to remember his morning wakeup call. It had been when...

The sound of a door slamming drew his attention. Colt glanced up to see Harper walking down the steps. She was already in her chef's uniform, looking fresh out of the shower. Her long, sandy blonde hair was still wet, not yet in her normal ponytail.

"Hello? Did I lose you?" Van's voice cut in.

"Hey, sorry. I gotta go." Pushing to his feet and reaching for his towel, he hung up as Van was shouting an obscenity.

She was almost out the door before he yelled her name. "Harper! Wait up."

She paused, her hand already on the knob. He got the sense she was avoiding him, and her actions in the next ten seconds would confirm or deny his suspicion.

He was almost to the door, dripping water behind him, when she spoke to him quietly. "What do you want, Colt?"

That was a fucking fantastic question. He had her attention, now what?

"I've tried to talk to you a few times, but it never seems to work out."

"Yeah, well, we're both kinda busy, aren't we?"

He wished he could see her eyes. Moving slowly as not to startle her, he reached to turn her around. Like in the garage weeks before, he gently pressed her body against the door, leaning in close enough to smell the lavender shampoo she'd used that morning.

He finally answered her question. "I'm not that busy. I think you're avoiding me."

She didn't deny it.

"What's the point? Neither of us are in a position to get distracted right now. I have a job to do and... so do you."

The way she said it bothered him. "And what job is it you think I have?"

"Don't play coy with me. I hear the girls talking in the kitchen every morning while they're avoiding eating the food I slave over for them," she lamented.

Fuck, he hadn't even considered that the contestants were interacting with her on their own. No wonder she was avoiding him. God only knew what they'd said in front of her.

"Listen, I can explain."

"Why? You don't have a damn thing to explain to me, Colt. I'm just the cook. A nobody." Her voice quavered.

He grabbed her arms, pulling her against his wet body. She melted against him like a wilting flower. Where the hell was the spunky chef who regularly put him in his place?

"Talk to me. What's going on?" He leaned back, hoping to figure out what was going on in that sassy head of hers.

The rising sun was now shining through the windows, making the tears in her lovely blue eyes sparkle.

She turned her head, refusing to look at him. His right hand cupped her face, forcing her to look back at him again. "Tell me. Something's wrong."

"How would you know?"

"That's a fine question. I honestly don't know how I know, but I do." He knew it at a gut level.

"It's nothing."

"Harper." He lowered his voice, demanding answers with one word.

"It's just... I listen to them all talking about you when

you're not there and... They are horrible women. All of them. Backstabbing you. Backstabbing each other. They lie, or at least I hope they do, because..." Her voice trailed off as she tried to look away.

"I'm so sorry you're getting caught up in this. I'll talk to Gavin and make the kitchen off limits for them. They can eat in the dining room and have Cecelia serve them."

His answer seemed to frustrate her instead of make her feel better. She was clearly exasperated when she answered. "That's fine, but that won't really solve the problem now, will it?"

"I guess it depends on which problem we're solving?"

They were both talking in circles now, unsure what to say, hell even what to think.

"I need to get up to the house. Everyone will be looking for breakfast soon."

"Give me a minute, and let me get dressed. I'll walk with you."

Colt released her, turning and rushing back to the table near the lap pool to throw on his pants and T-shirt. He'd only been gone a minute, but when he turned towards the door, Harper was gone.

"Goddammit."

If he suspected Harper had been avoiding him before the morning in the pool house, he knew for damn sure she was after. It had been four days. Four. Miserable. Days. Something had to change soon.

About an hour after he'd seen her in the pool house,

he'd laid down the law with the contestants. They were to stay out of the kitchen. He didn't want them talking to, complaining about, or even looking at Harper.

And about three seconds later, things had blown up spectacularly in his face with the cameras catching every sordid detail. Every single woman, including quiet Sophia, had badgered him about why he was defending another woman. The accusations flew until the stick-thin model, Cleo, had demanded to know why he gave a damn about the 'fat servant girl.'

He wasn't proud of it, but he'd lost his shit.

Even now, days later, he cringed thinking about how the viewing audience would lap up the drama when that episode aired after the holidays.

He didn't remember exactly what he'd said, only that before he could think, he'd picked up the nearest dining room chair and crashed it into the wall with all of his strength, punching holes through the drywall as he uncharacteristically lost his temper.

He'd only calmed when a frightened Harper had run in from the kitchen at the sound of the smash, freezing when she realized the entire room was glaring at her—half wanting to slap her, and the other half stunned into silence, their mouths agape.

He groaned, pretty sure that since they'd captured the scene from at least three camera angles, they had a good shot at induction into *The Guinness Book of World Records* as the most awkward thirty seconds in modern civilization.

He hadn't really understood the level of his anger himself, so when Gavin had pressed him for what the fuck was going on, he had no answers. All he remembered was threatening to walk off the project if Gavin even thought about firing Harper like the bitter women were demanding.

So now, days later, the occupants of the house were still in an uneasy truce of sorts. The women got digs in about the food when they could. Harper kept to herself, refusing to interact with anyone but the Finnegans. Gavin continuously set up situations that created escalating conflict; the bread and butter of reality TV.

As for Colt, he spent as much time alone as he could get away with, soul searching in a way he hadn't since he was a kid who'd set his sights on playing in the MLB. He went through the motions of fulfilling his filming obligation. Playing board games. Taking walks through the winter garden with different women on his arm. Watching movies in the theater. Steaming in the sauna. He tried to keep as many activities as a group as he could get away with. Safety in numbers, and all that.

But each day that passed, he felt more pressure to become intimate with at least the three women he'd be down-selecting in a few days. The rules, as they'd been set out, called for him to cut the field from six to three at the halfway mark. When the show had begun, he'd have bet his next payday on choosing Maya, Cleo and Kylie. But as he felt more pressure to sleep with them, he found himself wanting to choose the other three contestants if only to make the sexual pressure disappear.

And that made absolutely no sense to him, so he knew it would make even less sense to Gavin, who would, in turn, kick his ass for screwing up the show. The irony was not lost on Colt that he'd signed up to romance six women, presumably with the plan of overloading on debauched sex, and he had, instead, been technically abstinent for almost three weeks, well unless you counted Maya's blowjob.

Bill Clinton got away without calling that real sex.

That night, after a particularly scrumptious dinner of lobster bisque, shrimp scampi, and flourless chocolate cake, three of his favorites, Colt couldn't take it any longer. Feigning a stomachache, he retired early, leaving the women grumbling and the crew happy to have the night off. He went to his room just long enough to trade his suit in for a pair of jeans and a sweater. He grabbed his coat, wallet, watch and phone, hoping his plan was going to work.

He knew there were hidden cameras, but it couldn't be helped. He counted on the fact that no one could possibly view the thousands of hours of feed for the entire estate as he slipped down the back stairs, through the dark dining room and into the kitchen. His sense of disappointment at finding Harper already gone for the night was enlightening. It had taken him long enough to admit it to himself, but the plucky chef was at the heart of his problem.

Their verbal sparring aside, he'd finally put together the real reason he couldn't bond with any of the contestants.

He wanted Harper.

He'd wanted many women, of course, over the years. And he'd worked each and every one of them out of his system, which was exactly what he needed to do with her.

A few kisses… maybe a BJ or a quickie, and life could get back to normal. Well, as normal as living under a microscope for a reality TV show could get, anyway.

Undeterred, Colton stepped out the back door, taking long strides towards the darkened pool house. His mood lightened as he realized it would be better to seduce her there anyway. Less cameras. Fewer prying eyes.

He was about to let himself in the pool house when he noticed the lights were still burning bright in the stables. He wasn't surprised as he'd learned that the Finnegan's lived in the large apartment above the animals, much like Harper lived above the pool.

He turned the knob just as he heard the soft tinkle of Harper's laughter in the distance. Like being called by a homing device, he found himself changing directions, following the wafting sounds of camaraderie emanating from the barn.

He stopped in the shadows just outside the stable's open door leading to the well-lit paddock. He felt like an asshole for stalking her, but he was fascinated watching her working with the old caretaker, grooming a spirited Arabian. He was too far away to hear what they were talking about, but they chattered on like old friends.

Harper faced away from him, giving him the perfect view of her heart-shaped ass filling out the pair of jeans she was wearing perfectly. He found it interesting that she wore cowboy boots, the kind that looked well-worn versus the fancy fashion boots Cleo might wear on the runway. Add the ease with which she cared for the powerful animal, and he knew she'd spent time in a horse barn before.

That was a coincidence.

He'd grown up working on a Texas ranch only a mile outside of his hometown, mucking stalls for spending money. Old man Johnson had let him ride whenever he wanted, which had been often until a baseball came into his life. Then a bat had replaced saddles as his after-school companion. Hell, it had been over twenty years since he'd been on a horse.

Colt had been admiring the view for almost five minutes when the German Shepherd dog that had been sleeping near the water trough stuck his head up, alert and growling. Only when the canine took off running straight at him, barking as if he were fending off an intruder, did Colt finally step out of the shadows.

"Whoa there, boy. I'm just visiting."

He held out his hand as if to pet the barking dog, but not until Harper called out, "Wrigley, it's okay. Down, boy," did the protective dog back off. He still stood guard, ready to pounce if the new guy to the barn made a wrong move.

When he was relatively sure he wouldn't be attacked by Wrigley, Colton glanced up to find Harper glowering at him, all trace of her previous good humor having vanished.

"Hey, I saw the lights on and thought I'd check it out."

"Well, now you have, so you can go back inside now. I'm sure you're missed. It's almost bedtime." Her snappy snark had returned. He was relieved. It beat her tearful lack of confidence from a few days before.

"I'm sure everyone can get along just fine without

me." He braved moving closer. Wrigley still looked ready for a fight. "You're a natural with horses."

"And how would you know? Like you know anything about horses?" She scoffed, her hands on her hips.

"As a matter of fact, if you'd done a bit more research on me other than just my love life, you'd have found the stories about me growing up in Texas. My first paying job was mucking stalls for Johnson's Ranch about a mile from my house."

He grinned, happy to surprise her into silence.

He'd forgotten Charlie Finnegan was even there until the caretaker walked closer, holding out a pitchfork and a pair of gloves. "Care to relive a bit of your childhood, young man?"

At least the old man was still smiling, even if Harper wasn't. Suspecting it would piss her off, he grabbed the gear and grinned. "I'd love to help. It can replace one of my workouts."

He had just started scooping up a smelly pile of dung when he could swear he heard her swearing under her breath. Miss Gardener wasn't going to make this easy.

"What? No camera crew with you tonight?" She prodded, returning to her work.

He deposited the manure into a wheelbarrow and then broke open the fresh bale of straw using the pitchfork to shake the bedding into place for the lucky horse whose enclosure they were in.

"Naw. I gave them the slip. I needed to walk off that five-star dinner you served tonight."

He glanced up, watching for her reaction, not

expecting to find an evil smile as she added with glee, "I'm sure it was a big hit with all the ladies."

He'd suspected she'd been purposefully choosing dishes the contestants had nixed, but since it was creating such wonderful drama, Gavin had let it go.

Unaware of the veiled sparring his companions were engaged in, Mr. Finnegan gave him a gift. "You've helped me long enough. Let's get Dolly saddled up for your night ride. With the full moon, it's the perfect night for a ride around the lake."

Harper glanced his way nervously. What he'd give to get inside that adorable head of hers.

"I've changed my mind. I think I'll pass on riding tonight."

Colt saw his opportunity and jumped at it. "Actually, I think that's a great idea. Any chance I could tag along?"

He didn't ask Harper. He knew what her answer would be. He asked Charlie, who was only too happy to oblige.

"I'm relieved, to be honest. Ms. Gardener doesn't know the property well enough yet. Even with the full moon, I was worried about her riding alone. I'll go grab Prince and his saddle."

After they were alone, she pressed him. "Why are you doing this? Shouldn't you be in the house giving someone a massage or something?" The snark in her voice was morphing into nervous anxiety.

He took the high road. "I'd really like to ride, if it's not too much trouble. It's been almost twenty years and being out here... the smells... the sounds. It makes me almost homesick."

The funny thing was, in that moment, it was the truth. For a guy who traveled around two-hundred days a year for work, moving to a different hotel every few days, he rarely felt at home, even when he was at the loft in the city that technically was his home.

She didn't say yes. But she didn't say no, either. Colt helped Charlie saddle up the gelding, and within ten minutes, he swung himself up into a saddle for the first time in forever. The anticipation made him feel like a kid again as he waited for Harper to effortlessly pull herself up into the tall seat like the experienced horsewoman she was.

She looked as happy as he felt.

They started out slowly, finding the trail that ran along the white fence just before branching off into the bordering woods. It was significantly darker under the cover of trees that blocked the moonlight. They walked the horses in single file, the sounds of the forest surrounding them. Colt brought up the rear, enjoying the opportunity to study Harper on her steed as she led the way.

By the time they reached a clearing near the five-acre lake, all of the stress and anxiety from the previous weeks had magically receded, bringing a rare calmness. He normally lived his life at full speed, so the unexpected opportunity to ride in the moonlight with nature did his soul wonders.

Harper pulled her mare to a stop at the shore, sitting on her ride, looking out over the water. She looked cold in the November chill, her puffs of warm breath visible in the cool breeze. The light jacket she'd worn was not nearly hearty enough for the night wind off the lake. He stopped next to her, wanting to pull her into his arms to warm her. Not because he wanted to get in her pants. Well, to be fair, he did still want to get in her pants, but more so because the moment felt special.

"It was warmer here last night," she admitted.

"Thanks for letting me tag along. It's been a while since I've felt this at peace with the world."

She glanced at him, suspiciously. "Oh come on. With the money you make, you can afford to do anything you want to relax."

"True, but you'd be surprised how little I have left at the end of the year after I pay off everyone riding on me."

She looked pensive. "Is that why you're doing the show? You need the money?"

He barked a laugh. "Don't feel too sorry for me. I'm still in the top five percent earners in the MLB. To be honest, I got conned into doing the show in the middle of the playoffs when I wasn't paying attention to the fine print. Now I'm just trying to be a good sport about it all to avoid getting sued by the production company and Showtime for breach of contract."

Her eyes widened. "Can they do that?"

"You better believe it. I'm sure they'd like a crack at my bank account."

She didn't answer, looking back across the lake instead while his horse stretched down to make a snack of the remnants of last summer's long grass next to the clearing.

Colt dismounted, tying the reins to a low branch of the nearest tree and turning back toward Harper.

"What are you doing? We should go back now."

"Let's let them graze for a while. I'd like to find a few rocks to skip."

She looked uneasy with his request, glancing nervously in the direction they'd just come from as if she were tempted to take off again. He inched forward, trying not to startle the feral animal she suddenly resembled.

With a resigned sigh, Harper dismounted, and even though she needed no help whatsoever, he reached out to steady her, hands on her waist as her feet touched the ground.

They were close. He wanted to be closer.

She shivered in the cold, giving him the perfect opportunity to open his coat and step forward, sharing his body heat with her as he wrapped her in his arms, pulling her away from her horse and back against his chest. He'd half expected her to wiggle away, but she melted instead, throwing her head back until it rested on his shoulder as they looked out over the water.

Neither of them said a word, but her contented sigh spoke volumes in the quiet night. He froze, sure that any words he spoke or action he took would ruin what felt like a rare perfect moment. For a change, he didn't try to analyze it. He simply followed his instincts, nuzzling the woman in his arms, letting his lips find the sensitive juncture where her neck met her shoulder before nibbling his way slowly up to her left ear, sucking her earlobe into his mouth.

His first taste of heaven.

Colt's sleeping libido roared to life, demanding he make up for lost time. His brain, luckily, prevailed, forcing slow movements as his hands took on a life of their own. His fingers found her zipper, opening her coat to grant him access to her body as she subconsciously ground her ass against his expanding groin.

He knew he was doing something right when she fell harder against him, turning her body over to him as he explored her sexy curves. Her purr of contentment gave him the green light to latch onto her breasts through her shirt, squeezing her ample mounds, careful to pinch the protruding nips hard enough to send a jolt of excitement through both of them.

And then he made his first error. He spoke.

His, "Ah, Harper..." acted like a bucket of cold water thrown on the passionate couple. As if he were suddenly a hot poker, burning her, Harper jerked out of his embrace, bolting quickly away from her horse and Colton. By the time he caught up to her, she was fumbling to rezip her coat, her boots inches from getting wet in the placid lake.

"You shouldn't have done that," she accused, nervously breaking the silence.

"Why? It seemed like you were enjoying it."

She glanced his way as she spat angry words. "Screw you. Aren't you happy enough messing around with the contestants? I'd think you were getting so much booty that you wouldn't need to cheat on them with me."

There were so many problems with her assertion he didn't know where to start. He spun her body towards him so he could see her eyes in the moonlight.

"First, let me assure you, I've gotten zero booty, and even if I had, I'm not in a relationship with these women, so how the hell can I cheat on them?"

Her eyes widened. "I can't believe it. I knew you were a playboy, but I didn't peg you for a liar too. Well, no thanks. I'm not interested in being number seven on the list," she huffed, her spunky sass returning.

"What would you say if I told you that you were number one on the list?"

And he meant it. He wasn't interested in even playing Scrabble with the other six, let alone fucking them.

"What is this? Some kind of game?" As if she remembered something upsetting, she glanced around nervously. "Are you taping this? Are there cameramen out there trying to catch me acting like an idiot?"

"Oh for crying out loud, of course not! I wouldn't do that to you."

She didn't look convinced. "Why not? And maybe you wouldn't, but Gavin would in a heartbeat. I know the only reason he hasn't fired me is because he's hoping my being here is gonna make you do something stupid again like throw a chair through another wall." Her eyes softened with laughter as she started giggling. "I still have no clue why you did that by the way, but it was pretty fucking hilarious. You should have seen the look on everyone's face as I came running in. It was priceless."

"Yeah, real funny," he grumbled, running his fingers through his hair self-consciously.

Her tinkling laughter made it hard to stay embarrassed. "You should see their faces every night when Cecelia puts the food down on the table. You're sure to piss off at least one of them every single meal."

"That isn't hard, since between them there are only a

handful of things they won't bitch about. I mean seriously. Who doesn't like apple pie?"

Colt shared the joke. "It's un-American."

Their eyes locked in good-humored agreement. For the first time, he could tell she was tempted to lean closer.

Something was wrong with him. Gone was his Casanova confidence, replaced with a trepidation that had him actually nervous. It wasn't unlike the kind of anxious excitement he felt stepping up to the plate in a tight game, knowing something magical was about to happen. Only instead of his bat making the magic, he wanted it to be his other body parts that took charge tonight.

He met her halfway as she leaned into him. Their lips brushed softly, the kiss could almost be considered chaste if it wasn't for the feel of her taut nipples pressing against his chest. Nature took over, seducing the woman in his arms until they both had to come up for air.

Their foreheads pressed against each other as they caught their breath.

"Let's go back to your place," he almost begged.

She surprisingly didn't say no. "I'm not sure that's a good idea, Colton."

"It's the best idea I've had since I got here." He was back to placing small kisses on her cheeks and down to her neck.

"Why me?"

He froze. On the surface, he didn't have an answer. He had to dig deeper to uncover a hint of the truth. "Because... you're different. Real."

It was a stupid answer, but she seemed satisfied.

The atmosphere was heavy with emotion, so her grinning taunt took him by complete surprise.

"I'll race you back to the barn. If you beat me, we'll talk about it again."

She was already in motion, dashing back to her waiting horse and throwing herself on her back like a pro-rodeo rider. She was already cantering before he was even seated. He kicked his horse's flanks hard, determined to catch up to her.

"Come on, boy. I'm counting on you."

CHAPTER 4

Harper's heart was racing faster than Dolly was galloping. She could hear Colton's horse catching up to her. Her mind scrambled to make sense of all that had happened that evening. Her brain was screaming to just keep riding as far away as she could, but her heart seemed to be making all the decisions tonight.

It wasn't fair. She was just a normal girl, and the guy pursuing her was a fucking sex-god. She'd tried so hard to keep her distance, recognizing the dangerous pull to the larger-than-life persona the minute she'd met him. Colton King was a dangerous man. He may not be a murderer or thief, but sure as shit, he was doing a good job of trying to steal her heart.

She'd spent the last three weeks watching him from a distance. In the beginning, she'd expected him to be an arrogant asshole. When he'd turned out to be quite personable, she'd reasoned it was all part of his lover-boy routine. But even that wasn't adding up with his assertion of his celibacy where the contestants were concerned. Although, that might explain the growing hostility of the women, not against each other as she'd expected, but towards her.

Dolly had just come alongside the white fence that marked the final leg of their race. She had a big enough lead. She should race into the yard and declare victory, say her good-nights and stay the hell away from the American royalty. What she wanted to do was pull on the reins, let him pass and win her as his prize.

What she did do was slow just enough to let him catch up. She glanced sideways as he pulled along side her, his face hard with a competitive determination that surprised her. They raced the final hundred yards side-by-side, rushing into the paddock, their horses neck and neck.

"I won!" he shouted with a victorious laugh.

"It was a tie," she corrected.

The horses snorted and whinnied as they worked to catch their breath after their race. Colt dismounted first before coming to assist her. The second her boots hit the ground, he crowded her, trapping her between his hard body and her horse, leaning close enough that she could smell a hint of his shampoo and cologne. He was pure man, and she wanted him bad.

"Now, I think we had a deal, Ms. Gardener," he teased, so close she thought he might kiss her again.

"You didn't beat me."

"But I didn't lose either."

"You're splitting hairs."

"I'd like to split something else," he whispered against

her ear suggestively, sending shockwaves through every inch of her body.

"I can see I shouldn't have been worried about you." The voice of a strange man coming from the other side of her horse startled her and annoyed Colt.

He mouthed the words, "I'm sorry," to her just before releasing her. The cold evening air jolted her out of her sexual haze as Colton stepped away from her body.

"Van, what the hell are you doing back up here?"

She didn't know who Van was, but she owed him one. His arrival had saved her from making one of the biggest mistakes of her life. Harper turned, moving quickly to take off the saddle and put Dolly away for the night, so she could dash off to her room for some privacy. She couldn't help but hear the men's conversation as she worked.

"Gavin called earlier. Said you weren't feeling well, and he thought you could use a friendly face."

"So he called you?" She could hear humor in Colt's tone and suspected the men were friends.

"Har-har. Looks like you're feeling better. You gonna introduce me to your lady friend?"

"Nope."

"Ah, come on. I won't bite."

A movement from the corner of the stable caught her eye. It took Harper a minute to focus on the shadow, but when she did, her heart lurched, wondering just how much of their arrival the cameraman hidden in the corner had caught of their exchange. She couldn't risk being caught on camera in a compromising position. She'd watched enough reality TV shows to know that should that happen, she'd be turned into the villain of the season, and the contestants, who had been so rude to her, would be spun to look like innocent victims.

Charlie Finnegan arrived just as she was removing Dolly's bridle. She hated to impose, but she needed to slink away while Colt was still distracted.

"I hate to ask, but would you mind brushing her down for me, Charlie? I have a bit of a headache."

The wise man eyed her suspiciously, but if he suspected she was lying, he kept it to himself. "I don't mind at all, Miss Harper. It's just so nice to have folks using our stables again. I hope to see you back again tomorrow night."

She remained non-committal. "I'll try. Tell Cecelia goodnight for me."

"You aren't going to go up for a cup of tea like normal?"

"Naw, not tonight. I'm heading off to bed. See you tomorrow."

Harper left the stables through the far end, avoiding having to walk past Colton and Van as the men were deep in conversation. With any luck, she'd make it to her apartment before he noticed her gone.

Once outside, she hustled across the stone driveway, shortcutting through the expansive lawn. She didn't dare turn around, but she felt eyes on her, as if she were being watched. Whether by people or a camera, she wasn't sure which.

The lights were on in the pool house as they often were at this time of the evening. The production crew liked to hang out in the hot tub or at the bar, but tonight, a quick glance around found the space empty. She was relieved. She didn't want to talk with anyone.

Only when she was safely behind her closed door did Harper fall apart. The events of that night were threatening to overwhelm her. The intensity of her attraction to Colton alarmed her. If it were just sexual, she could understand, but it was so much more than that.

She'd been unprepared to like the guy. Between his playboy reputation, the fact that she knew next to nothing about major league baseball, and that she found it morally repugnant that he could even consider signing up to date six women at the same time while on camera, she was baffled as to how he'd broken down her defenses.

She just needed to hold out a few more weeks, and then they'd never see each other again. That couldn't be so hard.

She took off her coat and started undressing as she made her way to the bathroom. A nice hot shower would make her feel back to normal.

She turned the temperature to hot and got in, letting the water wash away more than the grime of the day. Willing her feelings of attraction for Colton to spin down the drain alongside the soap, she didn't get out until she felt calmer.

It was still early for bed, but she hadn't been sleeping well since her arrival. She threw on a pair of panties and one of the camisoles she slept in and dove under the covers of her king-sized bed. But sleep was elusive, her mind refusing to focus on anything but how his kisses had made her feel. It had to just be his fame that had made the way he held her feel different than any other embrace she'd ever enjoyed.

Twenty minutes was spent trying to put him out of her mind before she finally admitted defeat. Just one little hit and she knew she'd sleep better. Harper rolled to the edge of the bed, opened the drawer to the nightstand and pulled out her vibrator. She'd be lying if she didn't admit that masturbating had become part of her nightly routine since her arrival in Connecticut. The part that alarmed her was that, each night, she'd become more obsessed with pretending it was Colton King moving inside her. He was officially her number one fodder for her sexual fantasies.

Feeling warm, she threw back the covers, letting her legs fall open as she lightly rubbed the silicone dildo up and down her slit through the gusset of her cotton panties, feeling the wetness drenching the thin material.

God she was so wet already.

Harper closed her eyes, making it easier to envision it was Colt there touching her. Other nights she'd let her imagination run wild, dreaming of the things his sexy hands could do to her body. But tonight, she remembered reality. The feel of his lips on her neck. His sucking her earlobe into his warm mouth, latching on and nipping her with his teeth. The press of his hard body and even harder cock against her as they'd kissed passionately.

The real memories were even better than her dreams had been.

She pulled the waistline of the panties lower, exposing her pussy to the chilled room. The feel of the toy rubbing her clit was perfect as she used her left hand to snake under the fabric of her top, squeezing and then pinching her breast much like Colton had less than an hour before. She loved that her nipple was still tender, proof that she hadn't imagined the whole encounter.

"Christ, you're fucking beautiful like that."

Her dream felt so real. It was almost like... Her eyes flew open, frantically glancing to the door, and praying it had just been her imagination.

The fact that Colton King was standing inside her apartment was shocking enough. It was the engorged cock he had in his left hand that grabbed her attention and wouldn't let go.

"Don't stop, baby. I was really enjoying the show."

She was mortified. Her hand flew away from her pussy as if it were on fire, thrusting the glistening sex toy under her pillow in an attempt to pretend he hadn't seen what he had seen.

It didn't work. In fact, he was in motion, moving closer to the bed as their eyes locked. The temptation to glance lower at his erection was almost overwhelming. She needed to get him the hell out of there.

"I can't believe you broke into my room like this."

"I didn't break in. I knocked softly. You didn't answer. I tested the door, and it was unlocked."

"Don't play games with me, Colton. You know you shouldn't be here."

"I was worried about you. You ditched out so fast when Van showed up."

She tried to get angry. That was preferable to the irresistible pull he seemed to have on her.

"I left because I wanted to be alone."

"So you could fuck yourself while thinking about me?" His words were shocking, and unfortunately true.

"You're pretty sure of yourself, aren't you?" she retorted.

"But I'm right, aren't I?" he gloated, taking another step closer to the bed.

She refused to stoop to lying, no matter how badly she wanted to. She let her silence answer for her, regretting leaving the small lamp on.

He didn't stop until he was at the foot of the bed. She now had the perfect view of him in all of his glory, and boy was he magnificent. His shaft was long and thick, his balls hung heavy. Like the rest of the package that was Colton King. He was perfect.

Their eyes met, and she saw pure sexuality trying to devour her. God help her, but she wanted him so bad in that moment she almost invited him into her bed.

Thankfully, he had another idea. "Slip your panties off. I want to see all of you," he instructed, slowly nursing his dick. It felt like an order, and she complied.

Once her undies were thrown to the floor, he gave his next instruction. "Open your legs wider. I want to see everything."

She was glad she was lying down because she felt lightheaded as she followed his direction. Despite the fact they had yet to touch, there was no doubt in her mind that she was in the process of making love with Colton King. The sexual heat of his gaze alone almost made her self-combust.

"Now, slide your fingers through your slit. Make sure

to get them nice and wet for me." She did as she was told, in a trance, picking up speed as she rubbed her swollen clit until her hips started rocking up and down off the bed.

"Good girl," he growled, sounding almost pained. "Now, lick your fingers."

She faltered. Confused. "What?" she questioned.

"You heard me. Put your fingers into your mouth and tell me what you taste like."

Harper wanted to object, but even more, she wanted to hear him call her his good girl again. Moving in slow motion, she lifted her fingers to her lips, barely sticking her tongue out to lap at the wetness with timid licks.

"God, that's the sexiest thing I've ever seen. Open your mouth. Suck them in deeper now."

The parallel of her thrusting fingers in and out of her mouth to what she desperately wanted him to be doing with the hardness jutting out from between his legs was not lost on her. Her core contracted with a palpable need.

Why wasn't he coming into the bed? He had to know she was defenseless to reject him. He could take whatever he wanted from her, and she would gladly give it. She may regret it tomorrow in the light of day, but tonight, she was his.

A pained look furrowed his brow. "Take out your vibrator again."

She was not expecting their solo game to continue. "Colton..." she begged.

"I know, baby, but not yet. Trust me."

The odd thing was that she did.

Harper reached under her pillow, retrieving the

vibrator that was diminished by the presence of the real deal just feet away. Regardless, she held it, waiting... wanting him to take the lead in the dirty dance they were about to share.

"Slide it up and down. Get the shaft wet, but don't turn it on yet."

The faint sound of him stroking himself mingled with the louder sound of the toy sliding back and forth through her wetness. Several minutes passed as they each made the climb closer to their climax.

"Turn it on, but don't you dare orgasm. I want us to come together."

The vibration against her now sensitive clit almost threw her over the edge. She pulled herself back just in time to keep from exploding. She noticed his left hand had picked up speed, rapidly stroking his hard-on faster until pearly pre-cum glistened at the tip.

"Damn, I want to be on that bed."

"So why aren't you?" she invited.

He looked pained, like it was hard to talk coherently. She understood.

"Things are so complicated."

That was an understatement.

She was so close. She could barely form words. "Mr. Obvious."

He groaned at her attempt at humor, picking up speed with his hand until the sound of his skin slapping turned her on so much she thrust her hips up off the bed, pressing the hardness of the vibrator against her clit in an attempt to ease her ache.

"Ready?"

"To come?"

"Not yet. But when I say go, you're gonna fuck yourself with that bad boy. You're gonna thrust your hips up again and take the whole thing as deep inside as you can. And when you do, you're gonna know it's really me moving inside you."

What the hell was this man doing to her? He hadn't even touched her, yet this was the single most erotic experience of her twenty-five years. She waited with bated breath, having turned over control of her body to the man standing several feet away.

"Now! Shove it in."

She heard her own scream as the vibrating shaft filled her core, lifting her hips up to meet the thrust. Colton continued his directions to her through now gritted teeth as he fended off his own eruption. "That's it, baby. Fuck yourself hard and fast. Just like I'm going to do to you one day very soon."

That was it. The promise of his flesh being inside of her was the final push she needed to lose control. She closed her eyes, crying out his name as the explosion of ecstasy overcame her. She collapsed, exhausted, to the bed just as she heard Colton's grunts, closer now. He growled his own release just as she felt his first spurt of warm jizz land on her exposed tummy.

She opened her eyes in time to see how magnificent he looked as he succumbed to the fiery heat they'd stoked together. Harper watched as ropes of white spunk baptized her.

It took a good minute for her heart rate to slow to anywhere close to normal. As her brain came back on duty, she waited for the guilt and regret to arrive, relieved when it didn't.

A small smile played at Colton's lips. She recognized it as his up to mischief tell.

"Don't move."

"Ah... okay."

He reached towards her on the bed, using his pointer finger to slowly scoop up a glob of his ejaculate, making sure he didn't touch her body. She watched, enthralled, as his finger moved higher until he gave his next command.

"Open up for me."

Her jaw moved slowly, knowing what he was about to do was so naughty, yet loving the thought of drinking him.

His wet finger invaded her mouth, barely brushing the cream on her tongue. For the first time, she didn't wait for his direction. Harper clamped her mouth closed, sucking his finger clean as she swallowed his essence, tasting the tangible evidence of their unique tryst.

Like a gentleman, he left her long enough to retrieve a warm washcloth from the bathroom. He'd taken the time to tuck his cock back into his perfectly tight jeans.

He may not have touched her skin yet, but his cloth-covered hand gently rinsed the residue of their combined excitement from her body. After all they'd experienced together, for some reason, it felt odd to have his larger-than-life persona caring for her in such an intimate way.

It was only when he placed the cloth on the nightstand and looked down on her from above that her tears threatened. She was exhausted. She felt vulnerable. She was afraid.

She fought the urge to beg him to stay, knowing they'd already taken so many chances at being caught. But the thought of him going back to the main house—to his bedroom just feet away from six other women who were vying for his attention—turned her stomach.

"I'd stay if I could." He'd read her mind.

Finally, he touched her, cupping her face gently as he leaned in for a chaste kiss. "Sleep well, Harper. I'll see you in the morning, and if at all possible, I'll meet you in the stables again tomorrow night. It might be a bit later, but I'll be there if I can."

She nodded, too emotional at the thought of being the other woman in this sordid little affair, yet angry at the idea of sharing him at all with the miserable excuses for contestants.

She watched him cross the room, glancing back with a parting smile just before slipping out the door.

She probably should panic, after all, she didn't see how this complicated situation was going to turn out well for her. But in that moment, she was too relaxed. Too content. She closed her eyes and fell into the best sleep she'd had in weeks, dreaming of a man who felt just out of reach.

CHAPTER 5

Colton woke up feeling better than he had in... well, forever. For the first time in weeks, he had a path forward. He jumped out of bed and took a quick shower, anxious to meet with Gavin. He was glad Van had made the trip up after all. Better that he could tell both men together that he'd be breaching the contract. They could slap him with damages, and he'd gladly pay.

His failed foray into television would end up being a very expensive lesson.

Feeling like a new man, he hurried through the mansion on the way to the kitchen. The smell of her heavenly cooking greeted him before he even hit the first floor. Not for the first time, he admired the home they'd been renting, surprisingly sad that his time there might be coming to an end sooner rather than later.

He heard the voices as he came down the back stairs. Joking... laughing... He turned into the kitchen to find the room full of the production crew, plates stacked high with fluffy pancakes. And at the center of it all was a glowing Harper. He didn't care for the fact that it had been the cameramen and not him whom had put that joyful smile on her face.

"Good morning," he said, a bit too loudly.

The room fell into a hush as all eyes turned his way. The men, having been filming him for weeks, wished him a quick hello before going back to their breakfast.

But Harper stood frozen, unable to look away. He was a jerk for being relieved that she looked excited to see him. It stroked his ego to see the effect his arrival had on her.

Not wanting to tip their hand to the men in the room, Colton walked to her location, stealing a strip of bacon from the plate in front of her before whispering in her ear, "You're burning the pancakes, baby." He let his hand brush her curvy ass, cupping it lightly before stepping away.

Flustered, the chef got back to work, barely salvaging the last batch of flapjacks just before they could be called burned. Colton took a seat at the island where he had a perfect view of Harper preparing more food. He ate his hearty breakfast, anxious for the crew to leave them in some relative privacy.

Only Van had other ideas, arriving in time to sit next to Colt before he finished.

"So have you seen Gavin yet this morning?" Colt asked his agent between bites.

"He left me a note. Something came up. He needed to go into the city for a day or two. I can't believe he didn't tell you."

An uneasy feeling came over Colt, hoping the producer hadn't gone looking for him the night before only to find him MIA. But his disappointment was more than that. He wanted to get this game over with—once and for all—so he could move on with his life. With Gavin gone, it would drag things out. The crew wouldn't accept a shutdown of production without the producer.

Things went from bad to worse when Maya and Cleo, the shortest and the tallest contestants, arrived in the kitchen. It looked like they intended to take a seat next to Colton until he gave them the evil eye. They instead each grabbed an apple from a bowl of fruit and headed into the dining room.

"That's weird. Why didn't they sit down?" Van prodded.

Colt sat silent, but one of the crew was nice enough to answer for him.

"Colton banned the contestants from the kitchen earlier this week."

His friend and agent eyed him suspiciously, "And why would you do that?"

Colton and Harper looked at each other nervously.

"I think I see." His friend glanced pointedly between Colt and Harper before throwing his napkin onto his still half-full plate. "I'd like to speak with you in private, Colt."

"I'm not finished."

"Oh, I think you are." The men glared at each other, Colt understanding the real meaning of his friend's assertion.

Now that he'd made his decision to shut down the fiasco, he felt liberated. He didn't need to play nice with the women who were only looking for their fifteen minutes of fame and a chunk of his fortune. And he sure as hell didn't need to take shit from his agent.

"Actually, I think that's a good idea. Let's go out to the pool house. We can talk in the hot tub."

VAN'S TIRES spun on the loose gravel as his Audi tore out of the driveway. Their long, impromptu meeting had not gone well. Besides the fact his agent thought he was throwing away an important opportunity for his career, his friend hadn't understood why America's most eligible bachelor wasn't enjoying the carte blanche he'd been given to sleep with six beautiful women.

Since Colton barely understood it himself, he hadn't done a good job of explaining it either.

He just needed to get through today. Then Gavin would return, he'd nix the show and then... what?

The thought of returning to the mansion and pretending for the rest of the day repulsed him. The producers had set up an off-site adventure to New York City for the following day and he was supposed to be using today to discuss the options on camera. Since he alone knew he wouldn't be making that trip, at least not with the contestants along, he didn't feel the need to interact with the women further.

It was already two o'clock. He'd missed lunch, spending time arguing with Van instead. As tempted as he was to find Harper in the kitchen, he headed towards the stable instead. It was a beautiful day for a ride... sunny and warmer than in previous weeks. He needed to be alone so he could think.

The Finnegans were not to be found, but Colt didn't need Charlie's help. He saddled up Prince and headed off in the direction he and Harper had gone the night before.

In the light of day, he admired the peaceful landscape. Rolling hills, forests and pastures dotted the land. Opulent homesteads, like the one they were on, sprinkled the horizon. This was the kind of place men like him came to raise their family, not bang six women they barely knew. He even bet the schools were phenomenal, and the crime rate was non-existent.

He chuckled to himself. Since when did he start thinking about such things?

Alone on his ride, he had the time to evaluate the interesting question. He admitted it was hard not to think about settling down when every other member of the starting line-up was married with a family. He was the hold-out. The anomaly. Hell, at thirty-six, he was an old man in baseball. If he were lucky, he'd get two, maybe three, more seasons to try to break the doubles record, but then what?

The one thing he knew he didn't want was to continue stoking the fire of his notorious bachelor lifestyle. Like an old, comfortable shirt, that existence used to fit him perfectly. But this failed experiment had proven it had gotten too tight. Playing the field just didn't fit him anymore.

Looking out over Connecticut, he admitted the country felt ironically more like home than the dance clubs he used to haunt; a major revelation to be sure.

The one question he avoided the most was where did Harper Gardener fit into his new reality? He'd hoped a kiss and a quickie would work her out of his system, but that had backfired spectacularly. He'd lain awake for hours after returning to his room the night before, reliving how beautiful she'd looked pleasuring herself.

If their physical attraction had been all there was, he wouldn't be panicked, but more importantly, he'd had to face how much he loved just talking with her. Sparring with her verbally. As he'd pondered it in his bed the night before, the best adjective he'd come up with to describe her was real. She didn't put on airs to try to impress him. Hell, she barely even acknowledged his fame or fortune, let alone pandered to it.

The snort of another horse drew his attention. Up ahead he saw Dolly tethered to the same tree he'd used the night before. Where there was Dolly, he hoped there would be Harper.

Prince seemed to know where to go on his own, stopping right where he'd been the previous evening. Colt searched the area for the woman in question, finally finding her several hundred feet down the shoreline where a larger inlet had created the perfect picnic spot.

She obviously hadn't heard him approaching as Harper sat in the middle of the spread out blanket, her arms hugging her bent knees as she gazed out over the placid lake. He took a moment to observe her undetected. She'd let her hair down and long strands blew in the light breeze. He wanted to reach out and run his fingers through it.

Colt searched at his feet, picking up a half dozen

small rocks, before making his way to her. He knew the second she heard him coming, swinging around, a panicked look on her face.

"Oh for crying out loud, you scared the bejesus out of me."

"I can't help it if you weren't paying attention. I did arrive on a half-ton animal, after all."

She looked annoyed at his answer. "I didn't expect anyone. You should have called and warned me."

"I'd love to, but since I don't have your number..."

"A likely excuse," she countered, flustered, recognizing the truth.

Only now that he was closer did he see the small open basket on the blanket next to her. "Mind if I join you? I skipped lunch."

"I only brought enough for one."

"Hmm, well then you'd better get eating. That looks like a lot of food."

Were they really arguing over food?

Colton stepped in front of her, standing at the water's edge and pulled out one of the flat rocks he'd slipped into his pocket. The first one barely skipped even once, crashing into the water on the first bounce. Her soft laughter wounded his pride.

Trying again, his second attempt was much better. The rock bouncing twice before sinking farther out from shore.

"Is that the best you got?" she teased.

"I'd like to see you do better," he turned, holding out a flat stone for her to take her turn.

She looked conflicted until he smiled down at her, taunting her. She snatched the rock in a huff and pushed to her feet. Winding up, she let it go. Her rock bounced an impressive six times before sinking near the center of the lake.

"Okay, what gives?"

She smiled. "I grew up on a farm in Illinois. We had a lake on our property. I'm the unofficial queen of skipping rocks. Just ask my cousins."

"Prove it. Do it again." He held out the selection of rocks, and she chose again, this time increasing her skill set to seven skips.

Colton whistled. "Impressive."

He was tempted to reach out and pull her into his arms, but refrained. She was acting prickly again, and he'd need to bring down her defenses first.

Instead, he turned and took a seat to one side of her blanket, leaving space for her to sit next to him. Harper hesitated, but finally sat, careful not to get too close. A flock of wild geese flew overhead, late on their trek to the warmer south. After a few minutes of silence, they both started talking at the same time.

Him with, "I'm so glad I stopped by your place last night."

Her with, "Last night was a big mistake."

They both chuckled, easing the awkwardness of the moment.

"I've decided to pull the plug on the show," he declared. She glanced at him, surprised before he added. "I'd have already done it, but Gavin pulled a disappearing act on me."

"Colton, you don't have to do that just for me. I'm a big girl. I understand."

"I'm glad somebody does."

"Seriously, Gavin is gonna be really pissed, not to mention the rest of the crew who will get sent home early."

Colt was surprised by her objection. "I thought you'd be relieved after all the crap you've had to put up with from the women."

It looked like she was biting her tongue to keep from saying something. He waited her out. "Obviously, I'm not sorry to see the contestants and cameramen leave. It's just..."

She'd stopped short of saying what he'd been thinking about on the ride there. Once the show ended, what happened to them?

The topic was too heavy for the sunny afternoon. He diverted the subject to the remaining food packed in the small basket between them. "I'm starving. What do you have to eat in here?"

CHAPTER 6

Harper was hiding. She wished she had the courage to do what she knew was right, but she'd been sitting in her car in the dark garage for almost an hour now, unable to start the engine and drive away.

How had things gotten so out of control? A few months ago, she'd moved in with George. She'd had her dream job in a popular NYC restaurant. She'd been so sure she was happy.

Now, looking back with the distance of time, she questioned her sanity. George had treated her like shit, both at the restaurant and at home. His arrogance had known no bounds, and she'd been too impressed by his credentials to call him out on it.

Now weeks later, she'd met a man who was a thousand times more famous, rich and successful than George would ever dream of, and yet Colton had turned out to be the kind of man romance novels were written about.

They'd spent the entire afternoon together, talking easily from one topic to the next. She'd waited to find something—anything—to change her opinion of him, but in the end, as they'd returned the horses to the stables, she'd panicked realizing how hard she'd fallen for the handsome baseball player. Watching him court the other women had been hard enough. How the hell was she supposed to just say goodbye and walk away, never to see him again?

What it came down to, their sexual attraction aside, there was no way Colton King ended up with a girl like her. He was American royalty, and she was the girl next door. He should marry an exotic princess or an A-list actress.

Marry. There she went again. Blowing the last few weeks up into something that was just a figment of her imagination. Colton was a confirmed bachelor. The chances of him settling down with anyone, let alone her, were about the same as George Clooney or Matthew McConaughey.

But didn't they both get married?

She shook her head. This wasn't helping. She should start the car and drive away. The problem was she didn't know which way to point the car—back to NYC or all the way back to Illinois? Her family would be thrilled to have her home again, but she knew without a doubt, she would regret giving up on her dreams later in life.

The sudden flash of the overhead florescent lighting hurt her eyes. She covered her face with her hands as she slouched down in her seat, desperate not to be seen. Her pupils adjusted to the light enough to open her eyes just in time to see Colton approaching her Honda, a worried look on his face. Once he saw her car was still there, she expected him to turn around and retreat, but he didn't stop until he stood next to the driver's side door. Just in the nick of time, she reached and flipped the door lock.

"What the hell are you doing sitting out here in the dark? I've been looking all over for you." He leaned down, pinning her with a seething glare. His anger surprised her.

"I'm going back to New York," she replied as she finally sat up.

"No you're not. At least not yet. Open up the door."

Harper's pulse spiked. Didn't he know that she wanted to press that button more than anything else in the world? But then what? She'd only get hurt worse the more time she spent with him.

"Harper Louise Gardener, open the damn door."

"How the hell do you know my middle name?"

"I know lots about you. You need to seriously be more careful about what you post on social media. Guys don't need to know what kind of panties you wear."

He'd been stalking her Facebook account? More importantly, she was sure there was at least a twinge of jealousy in his tone.

"I didn't think my choice in underwear was top secret."

"Yeah, well..." He was flustered, running his fingers through his hair. "I mean it. Open the damn door."

The second the click of the lock sounded, he swung it open, reaching in to pull her to her feet. Within a second, she was trapped, her back against the car, her front flush with the muscular chest she'd admired as he swam.

"Why the hell are you leaving? I told you, when Gavin gets back tomorrow, I'm calling it quits on the show."

"Right. So I'll get fired, with everyone else on the crew."

Her answer flustered him. "Okay, maybe I hadn't thought about that, but it doesn't matter. You don't need to leave. We have the estate through the end of the year."

God, how she wanted to stay here and play house with him. It was a fairytale mansion. A fairytale man.

The problem was, fairytales weren't real.

He didn't wait for an answer. He moved her aside to grab her hastily packed bag from the back seat and closed up the car. Unlike their initial trek to her apartment on her first night there, tonight he grabbed her hand as they left the garage. Neither of them spoke as they walked across the expansive yard, passing by several barn cats out for their nightly stroll.

So much of being here reminded her of the best parts of growing up in the country. Instead of making her homesick, it just made her doubt her life decisions. She'd been so positive she belonged in a major city, but she wasn't so sure any more.

The pool house was thankfully quiet as she retraced her steps from an hour before. Colton needed both hands to carry her heavy bag up the stairs. As she followed him, she couldn't take her eyes off his perfect ass just inches away. They'd be alone again in less than a minute. Would he be a gentleman and leave her like he had after their ride that afternoon, or would he pick up where they'd left off the night before?

She truly didn't know which option scared her more.

She didn't have to wait long for an answer. The second the door closed behind them, Colt threw the lock and turned to pounce on her. Unlike the night before where they had gone hands-free, tonight they were like magnets, unable to keep their hands off each other. Their lips locked, tongues dueling in the kind of kiss that made her knees weak.

He didn't need to instruct her. She knew instinctively what he wanted, unbuttoning his long-sleeve dress shirt and pressing it off his shoulders just as he set them apart long enough to pull her frilly top over her head and throw it to the floor on top of his shirt.

Their pants were next. It took several minutes since each was unzipping by touch only, unwilling to stop making out long enough to properly disrobe.

Only when the back of her knees hit the bed did she realize he'd been slowly shuffling them away from the door. As soon as she'd pulled his T-shirt over his head, Colton shoved her torso away from him, making her bounce as she landed with a plop on the bed, her feet still dangling towards the floor.

Their eyes met as his fingers worked their magic, pulling off her shoes and socks, leaving her lying below him in only her bra and panties. He finally slowed things down, leaving her to catch her breath as he took one step back, allowing her to watch him take off his own shoes and socks, leaving him in only his boxer briefs.

They hadn't spoken a word since they'd left the garage, but in that moment, she could see her own insecurities reflected back at her through his eyes. How could that be? The guy was a freaking Casanova. She told herself this was business as usual for him. It was the only way she'd have a chance at not being destroyed when he walked away from her as he had hundreds of women before her.

"What are you thinking about?" He frowned. When she didn't answer, he added, "Whatever it is, don't. You looked sad there for a second."

She was sad. But she was also committed. Unless the pool house caught on fire, she was going to make love with Colton King. She might as well enjoy it. She'd have plenty of time to live with her regret of losing him later.

The second she let a smile play at her lips, he relaxed again, turning playful.

"Now, I think you have a few too many clothes still on. I need to get another look at you—up close and personal tonight."

She chuckled. "You were pretty up close and personal last night too, if I recall."

His fingers hooked in the elastic of her panties, slowly pulling them down her legs until they were in his hand. Harper almost self-combusted when he held her discarded intimate apparel to his nose and took a deep drag. The feral groan that followed went straight to her core.

Colton fell to his knees, reaching forward and pulling her bottom closer to the edge of the bed. He lifted her feet, placing them on his bare shoulders, spreading her open as he dove forward.

His tongue connected with the bottom of her slit, lightly licking upward in short laps that only fueled her passion for him. He teased her as he tasted her, using his fingers to hold her nether lips wide, exposing her shaved pussy. Harper closed her eyes, letting the ecstasy wash over her as he plunged a finger inside just as he sucked her swollen nubbin into his mouth.

He was prepared for her hips rising off the bed, holding on to her bent legs as handles as he ate her out with gusto.

Only after her first orgasm did he slow things down, building her up again. He was patient. So generous as a lover. She tried to only focus on the physical nature of their tryst, but with each passing second, their emotional bond grew stronger until Harper felt hot tears threatening.

He was so tuned into her body that he knew the exact second she tipped into her next climax, inserting his thumb in her most private hole while shoving several other digits in her pussy. The suction he applied on her clit was the final straw.

She was sure they had to hear her screaming his name up at the main house. The tears that had threatened earlier spilled down her cheeks. She'd never come so hard in all her life and was pretty sure it was a fluke. A once in a lifetime high.

Harper lay panting on the bed, recovering. She vaguely heard Colt moving around the room, but she was honestly too spent to crack her eyes open to see what he was doing.

It wasn't until he lifted her into his arms to carry her to the bathroom that she forced herself to perk up.

"You can put me down. I can walk." Suddenly self-conscious of her weight, she envisioned him throwing his back out and her being personally responsible for ending his career. Even she knew that was a bit melodramatic, and she started to giggle.

"I love the sound of your laughter."

She was about to make an awkward joke about her size-ten body when he stepped into the bathroom, and all jokes left her brain. He'd brought several candles in from the bedroom and lit them, placing them strategically around the space. He'd drawn her a bath and, from the smell of the steam wafting up, had put in her favorite lavender oils.

Colton set her feet on the fluffy rug and reached for the back clasp of her bra. His breathing hitched just before he pulled the fabric away, getting his first look at her heavy breasts. They were the only benefit of carrying a few extra pounds, and from the sparkle in his eyes, Mr. King approved.

Like her pearl before, her hard nip found its way into his mouth. Teeth grazed the tender tip, sending electric shock waves through her entire body. It was a good thing he still supported her, or she might have toppled to the floor in a pool of melted goo.

"Oh God, that feels so fucking good." Her words encouraged him. Both his hands cupped and squeezed as his mouth migrated to her other peak, leaving a trail of wet kisses in the valley between her mounds.

He feasted on her as she clung to him, daring him to try to get away. The scruff of his day-old beard scratched her sensitive skin, yet she welcomed the sensation as it helped prove she wasn't just dreaming.

"Colton..." she pleaded, "I need you."

He released her pebbled nipple only to ravage her lips instead. As they embraced, skin-on-skin for the first time, she lowered her hands to the waistband of his briefs, pulling them down to expose his steely erection.

Harper tried to fall to her knees to repay the oral favor, but Colton stopped her.

"I won't last a hot minute if you do that, baby. Let's get in the tub instead."

"But..." she tried to argue.

He lifted his fingers to her lips to shush her. She picked up the scent of her cream on his digits. "No arguments. I want to talk."

Her heart rate spiked, afraid of what he'd say. He helped her sink into the hot water, turning on the whirlpool jets before crawling into the oversized tub behind her. She let him settle against the end cushion before scooting back until their bodies locked together like puzzle pieces.

Every part of his body was muscle. He was lean and fit. Athletic and hard. Colton King was perfect.

And yet, as he held her in his embrace, massaging her body as he let his hands roam, memorizing her curves, she sensed a tenderness she hadn't anticipated. She'd expected full-out intensity from the larger-than-life man, so this romantic version of a lover humbled her.

Colton nuzzled her neck, nipping and licking, kissing and sucking. Flaming her internal heat higher. In return, she snaked her arm between their bodies, wrapping her hand around his girth, caressing and squeezing, kneading and pinching until he hissed against her ear. She knew he was close to exploding when his mouth clamped down on her shoulder so hard she whimpered as he growled the sexiest sound she'd ever heard.

Like the night before, Colt started barking orders. As a modern woman, she should be offended, but in that moment, the sheer carnality of his voice sent jolts of pure passion through every inch of her body.

"Turn around. Face me."

As large as the tub was, it still took some maneuvering to reverse directions. The loss of their skin-on-skin connection was overshadowed by the ability to look into his gorgeous caramel brown eyes. He pulled her to him, opening her legs to wrap them around his waist.

The second the tip of his erection came into contact with her pussy, they each trembled, overwhelmed by the emotional connection.

He brushed a stray lock of her long hair away from her face as he asked a serious question.

"Please tell me you're on the pill. I don't understand it, but I need to come inside of you so bad."

Part of her wanted to tease him, but the moment seemed too important for that. "I am," she whispered.

He didn't wait another minute. Colton lifted her in the water until his cock was poised to impale her, holding her there so long she had to prompt him.

"I'm ready." Her voice was breathy. The flames from the candles flickered in the otherwise dim room, casting what felt like a magical hue over them. Slowly, he eased her lower, letting gravity help impale her with his cock. The stretch was magnificent, wide enough to hurt just right.

The water had washed away some of her slickness,

but she was more than excited enough to accommodate his girth. When her ass finally sat on his legs, the entire length of him buried inside her, a calmness filled her heart. It helped her relax and enjoy the feeling of him moving, lifting her only to release her again.

Colton was in control of her body and soul. In that moment, she'd do anything to make him keep the lustful gaze on his face for the rest of his life, or at least until the other six women could take note at breakfast the next day.

The pace of his thrusts became erratic the closer he got to his climax. The extremely fit man was breathing heavily as he chased his high. Water splashed higher as their rhythm changed tempo. By the time she felt his cock contracting, she was too far gone herself.

Colton grabbed her hips, pressing her down onto his erection as he grunted his sexy growl, tipping into his own pleasure. She wasn't far behind, the heat of the ropes of cum branding her from the inside.

She collapsed against him, wrapped in his arms, connected in the most intimate way. His hands groped her, exploring even as they caught their breath. They washed each other slowly, massaging sore muscles while mapping each other's body. By the time his cock had softened, slipping out of her, the water was starting to cool.

They went through the motions of preparing for bed, touching every chance they got. They blew out the candles and returned to the bedroom; it was getting late. She half expected him to get dressed and leave, yet she desperately wanted him to stay—to sleep with him, snuggled close, even if for just one night.

She almost cried with relief when he pulled back the covers and slid in next to her. They clung to each other in the darkness, petting until they each became drowsy. She didn't want to go to sleep and waste even a minute of their time together.

He read her mind. "Don't worry. I'm not leaving. At least not until morning."

She relaxed in his arms. "I think I'll take a little nap then."

CHAPTER 7

The sun was peeking over the horizon when Colton finally dragged himself out of Harper's bed. What he wanted to do was stay there for a week with Cecelia delivering food and drink to sustain them. But what he was going to do was find Gavin and put an end to the charade of a reality show.

Once he was dressed, he took a minute to watch over Harper, enjoying the peaceful look on her face as she slept. It was another first for him. He'd racked up many in the last few weeks. Hell, just in the last twenty-four hours he'd ridden horses with a woman, joined her on an impromptu picnic, treasured cuddling all night and now dreaded leaving her. All firsts for the confirmed bachelor.

The room smelled like sex, but it was no wonder considering they'd made love every few hours throughout the night. He leaned down to kiss her brow, hoping he could find Gavin and be back before she even woke up.

He pulled the door closed quietly behind him as he

took the stairs down to the pool house. The two-story expanse was still dark, making the glow of a cigar stand out. The shadowy silhouette turned into Gavin as Colton got closer.

He was relieved. "I'm glad you're back. We need to talk."

"Damn straight we do. I see you've been busy while I was away."

Colton wondered how the producer even knew he wasn't asleep in his own bed. Regardless, he didn't want to have this conversation so close to the sleeping Harper. He suspected there would be raised voices involved and wanted to spare her.

"Let's go up to the house. We can put on some coffee," Colton suggested.

"No, I think we best stay here. I wouldn't want anyone else to listen in."

"Well, they'll find out soon enough that I'm out. I know you'll need to fine me for breach of contract, but I accept that's what I need to do."

Gavin pinned him with an unreadable glare. "I'm afraid it isn't that simple."

"Sure it is. I was under contract. I'm breaking it. You'll fine me and we'll call it a day."

"Just like that?" he asked flatly. Colton didn't know how to reply, so he kept quiet until Gavin crossed the line. "She must be some piece of ass to throw the whole show down the fucking tube for her."

As the producer's offensive words registered, Colton grabbed him by the collar and yanked him to his feet, easily manhandling the smaller man. "You'd better watch yourself, Wallace, or you'll end up with my fist in your face."

The bastard had the nerve to flash a determined smile. "Go ahead. That'll make for a better show."

"I told you, there is no show." Then it hit him. He glanced around, expecting to find a cameraman lurking in one of the shadows, relieved when they appeared to be alone.

Gavin's grim smile kept him on edge. " You really should have read the fine print better." He paused before adding, "And so should have Harper."

His first alarm bell started going off. Colton shoved the wiry man away from him, trying to intimidate him. "Leave her out of this. This isn't her fault. I never should have signed up for this fucking circus in the first place."

"On that we can agree, but there will be no leaving Harper out. In fact, she's ending up to be the star of the show."

Colt grabbed him again, lifting the shorter man until his feet dangled like a runt about to be beaten up on the school playground. A hot rage he didn't understand coursed through his veins. He had always been competitive, but for the first time in his life, he wanted to do true harm to another human being.

Through gritted teeth, he corrected the producer. "You air anything that hurts Harper and you'll never work in sports journalism again. You said it yourself. I'm sports royalty. You fuck with Harper and I'll call in every favor I need to in order to make sure I destroy you. Got it?"

A drop of perspiration ran down Gavin's forehead. It was the only indication his threats had impacted the other man. The asshole's expression remained blank—unwavering.

"The law is on my side on this one, Colt. I have a binding contract with you and Harper. Every minute of the footage I've collected, both audio and video, are mine to do with as I please."

It took all of his effort to keep from ripping the little weasel's head off his shoulders. Needing space, Colton took a step forward and threw Gavin back into the poolside chair with such velocity the man almost tipped backwards.

The cigar he'd been smoking had fallen to the floor and was rolling away. Colton shuffled forward and stomped on it so hard it crumbled into shreds beneath his grinding shoe.

"That was a damn Cuban, you asshole."

"I'll buy you a fucking truck-load of them if you just walk away from this," Colton offered, appealing to the guy's greed.

"Like I said, it's not that simple. We have airtime we need to fill. Sponsors we've sold prime-time ad space to. They're expecting prime-time numbers. I was panicking, because they sure as shit weren't gonna get viewers with your choir boy routine."

Colton felt trapped. He needed to go to his room and re-read the contract again. There had to be an out clause somewhere. It would be an expensive lesson to learn, but he'd made twenty-two million last season. He could afford it.

"Fine, I'll go call my lawyer and get him working on burying you." He turned, taking angry strides towards the exit.

Gavin yelled out, taunting, "I sure hope Harper can afford a good lawyer too."

Colt stopped in his tracks, a ball of dread forming in the pit of his empty stomach. He spun, pinning Gavin with a death glare. "I told you to leave her out of this. She has nothing to do..."

"Oh for Christ's sake, how can you keep a straight face as you say that? Harper has everything to do with what's been going on around here. I admit. I didn't see it until you threw the chair through the wall earlier this week defending her. Looking back, it was so obvious, although I had to pay a crew back in the city a small fortune to comb through the hundreds of hours of camera footage looking for encounters we'd missed in the production van. To think, you guys met the very first night."

"How did you..." His voice trailed off.

There are cameras everywhere but in the shitter.

They'd warned him.

"You have cameras in the garage?"

"I admit, we didn't put those there. They were installed for security on the high-end vehicles, but, yeah... there are cameras in the garage."

He had a sinking feeling. "The stables?"

"Of course," Gavin scoffed.

Colton dreaded digging any deeper, but then he realized if he didn't ask now, he could always wait and watch it on national television with millions of other viewers instead.

The men glared at each other, Gavin's expression almost daring him to ask.

"And... the pool house."

"Yes."

He was short of breath, pushing down his anxiety. "I swear to God, if you have a camera in her bedroom, I'm gonna kick your ass."

Gavin made him wait almost thirty seconds, before finally acknowledging, "Actually, there are two there."

Colt's right fist connected with Gavin's left cheekbone exactly two seconds later. The asshole went down like the pussy he was. Colton wasn't even close to being finished with him, leaning over to pick the prick off the floor just so he could punch him in the stomach.

Before he could move in to deliver a third helping of whoop-ass, two previously unseen guys tackled him from behind and tried to wrestle him to the ground.

Colton fought them off, taking his rage out on them until the men he recognized as his assigned cameramen raised their hands in surrender.

And that was the moment he realized that even their private conversation and the physical altercation from this morning were now memorialized forever on film.

He was going to be skewered by the press for this. Hell, if the three men decided to press charges, Gavin may have to send a camera crew along to the county lockup with him. That ought to garner phenomenal ratings as they chronicled Colton King's travels through the

American court system as he was booked for assault and battery.

He needed to think. He needed to get Harper the fuck away from the cameras. He needed to...

"Now that you got that out of your system, why don't you sit down? I have a proposal for you."

"No thanks. I got into this mess listening to one of your crazy proposals."

"It's a bit late now to try to sweep all this under the rug." Gavin's nose was bleeding. He stopped talking long enough to grab a towel from the nearby table, using it to try to stanch the bleeding as he continued. "There's no way we have enough footage worth using to stick with our original plan. Short of Maya's blowjob, you've barely even touched anyone but Harper."

Colton groaned. Of course they had the BJ on tape. Ironically, his first thought wasn't how it would look to the millions of viewers who might potentially see it on an upcoming pornographic episode. Instead, he worried about how Harper would react, knowing it would hurt her.

"Get on with it," he said impatiently, angry that he had to spend another ten seconds listening to the jerk, but not really in a position to walk out either.

"I know it wasn't what we planned, but your time with Harper is like gold for the show. Your time together in the stables, out riding and even the picnic at the lake..."

Fucking hell.

"...only thing better is if you'd had sex out there, but I get it... it was too cold."

Colton interrupted him. "There has to be something. Some other way. I'm not dragging her into this."

"She dragged herself into this. She did everything but poison the women. Don't forget. She signed a similar contract. She knew the score on the cameras."

The ball of anxiety in his gut exploded. Had Harper known there were cameras in all of the places where he'd thought they'd had privacy? Surely she hadn't seduced him on purpose? His heart physically contracted, rejecting the thought of her possible betrayal, but his logical brain wouldn't let the idea go.

The irony of waiting thirty-six years to finally fall hard for a woman, only to have her turn out to be using him like he'd used hundreds of women before her, wasn't lost on him. There had to be a mistake.

"Colton?" Her voice called to him from a few feet away. She sounded so confused... almost fragile. His instinct was to protect her from the bullshit that was going down, but his self-preservation kicked in, throwing up a protective wall between them.

He swung to confront her, only to find her standing there in a terry cloth robe, looking adorably vulnerable. Her long locks were having a bad hair-day, having been tossed around all night long. But it was her lips that he couldn't stop looking at. They were pink and still swollen from their passionate kissing. They'd looked beautiful stretched wide around his cock around three that morning.

"You should go back upstairs."

"But what's going on? I heard voices and then a crash."

He was aware that the cameramen he'd attacked were no longer in sight which meant they were back behind the lens, hiding away as they taped every word... every syllable.

Colton felt trapped. He needed to be alone, away from prying eyes just to think. There had to be a way out of the mess he'd gotten into.

"You need to go home, Harper. Back to New York."

"New York? What's going on. Why are you sending me away?" Tears spilled down her cheeks in seconds, taking remnants of yesterday's mascara with them. She was either genuinely hurt, or an Oscar-worthy actress. The problem was, he didn't have the time to ferret out the truth right now, and sure as shit, he didn't want to duke things out with the beautiful chef with an audience of millions.

"It seems I didn't read the fine print of the contract well enough. I have a lot of shit to sort out. I don't know what's going on yet, but I will find out." It was a statement, but he failed miserably at hiding his resentment for being put in this position. He didn't miss her flinch as she internalized his words.

Gavin interjected. "I told you, she can't leave. She's under contract."

Colt turned back towards the producer. It was easier to face that man's anger than Harper's tears.

"She's the fucking chef, not one of the contestants."

"Harper signed the same contract that the camera crew and the Finnegans did. Hell, even your agent, Vencinti, had to sign one just in case he was caught up in a scene on one of his visits, I'd have the right to use the footage."

"Goddammit." Colt dragged his fingers through his hair nervously. He felt truly trapped. Had he known what was waiting for him at the bottom of the steps, he might have tied the bed sheets together in Harper's room and had the two of them shimmy down from her window to make a run for it to her Honda.

The sound of Harper crying softly made it impossible to think of anything else but wanting to comfort her, but that wasn't what she needed from him the most in that moment. He knew what she didn't. That their special night spent together in her room would soon be turned into the main attraction of the three-ring circus that was in town. He needed to protect her.

You need to protect yourself, King.

He closed the distance between them, fighting an internal war as he set his half-baked plan into motion.

"I'm sorry things played out this way, Harper. I really am. But, it's for the best that you go back to the city, and let me sort things out here."

"You want me to leave?"

Technically, he wanted them both to leave, but he held his tongue. "I do."

She flinched, visibly shaken. He wanted to believe she was an innocent bystander, caught up in the craziness of the reality show, but even if that were true, it only made what was going to happen when the show aired that much worse.

"Give me your number. I'll be in touch when the dust settles."

Soft cries gave way to her anger as she pushed away from him. "Don't do me any favors. I wouldn't want to mess up your 'one and done' dating philosophy."

It was his turn to flinch at her angry words. He hated the thought of her leaving thinking she'd just been another notch in the bedpost of a playboy. He forced a deep breath, thinking through his options, and realized he hated her staying anywhere near Gavin's cameras even more. They'd given the production crew more than enough fodder for their game. He already faced a hell of a legal battle. He needed to focus on that. It was the best way to protect Harper, even if she didn't understand it at the moment.

"I'm sorry you feel that way, but if that's the way you want it."

"Nothing is the way I want it!" she shouted, pushing away from him with a sob.

He watched her race up the stairs to her bedroom, slamming the door behind her. He sensed Gavin in his peripheral view. It took all his willpower to keep from taking his frustration out on the producer, but they'd just delivered a heart-wrenching scene for the cameras. He didn't need to add another assault to his resume.

Colton turned and pinned Gavin with a serious glare. "I'm going back to the main house. I'm grabbing my phone and my copy of the contract, and then I'm going into my bathroom because apparently that is the only place in the entire property I have any assurance of any privacy. I need you to help Harper carry her stuff down to her car, and send her on her way back to New York. You aren't to threaten her. You aren't to touch her. Hell, you aren't even to talk to her. I want her safely away until I get this all sorted out. You got it?"

Gavin was staring at him, that same unreadable look on his face, until he finally nodded. "I sure as hell hope you know what you're doing."

Colt took off for the door, unwilling to verbalize that he hadn't the damnedest clue.

CHAPTER 8

"Wait, you just took the wrong exit," Harper corrected her best friend, Vivian.

"Will you relax? I know where I'm going." Viv's reassuring smile was annoying. Didn't she know the world was an evil place?

"This is the stupidest thing you've ever conned me into doing," Harper said, and she meant it.

Her friend reached out to smack her arm playfully. "My couch begged me to get you out of the apartment, even if it is just for a little bit. You've been parked there for two weeks straight, only getting up for bathroom breaks and to pay the pizza delivery guy."

"That's not true. I ordered Chinese and Thai, too."

Viv chuckled. "I stand corrected. All I know is if I don't get you moving again, your next delivery will be a new wardrobe in the next bigger size."

"Gee, thanks. Nice way to tell me I'm getting fat."

Her friend suddenly got more serious. "Fat, no. But I

just can't sit by and watch you be so sad. You should be bouncing back by now."

Harper bit her tongue, knowing it wouldn't do any good to argue. She knew in her heart there would be no bouncing. She'd already jumped headlong, heart and all, only there hadn't been a safety net to catch her. It was an expensive lesson to learn at the young age of twenty-five, but you play with the big boys, and you go splat.

No, there would be no bouncing back for Harper.

"He still hasn't called?" Viv asked for the hundredth time since Harper had shown up sobbing on her friend's doorstep.

"I told you. He isn't going to call."

"I think you're wrong. You said yourself, the producers are forcing him to finish filming. He's probably just protecting you by not calling you while he's being filmed."

"Don't forget, I pumped Gavin for more information before I left. He finally admitted that they have us recorded doing the nasty in half of the positions of the Kama Sutra. Trust me, nothing he could say on the phone could make things worse. The best part is, in just a few weeks, my parents are going to have a front row seat to the crash and burn of my X-rated love life. He isn't calling because he's done with me. I never asked, but based on the stories on the Internet, I'm somewhere around girlfriend number 237."

"Okay, you're exaggerating again, and I still say you should give him the benefit of the doubt."

"Since when are you a Colton King fan?"

Viv smiled. "Since my best friend fell in love with him."

"I think you missed the part where he broke my heart."

"How could I miss it? You've been crying on my couch for two weeks."

"Sorry. I'll pack up—"

"Stop! I'm not complaining. I'm just worried."

"So that's why you dragged me out to Timbuktu?"

"No, I dragged you out so you could get some fresh air and remember there is a whole, big world out here. And because I can't carry the Christmas tree by myself."

"We've passed by a dozen places selling Christmas trees, you know," Harper retorted.

Her friend smiled. "I know, but there is this one farm that has the best trees, and we get to pick out our favorite, and they'll cut it down for us."

"I never pictured you as the Martha Stewart type."

"Yeah, well there's a first time for everything. Why don't you take a nap? I'll wake you up when we get there."

At least a nap would stop the depressing conversation about how fucked up her life was. She reclined the bucket seat of her friend's sedan and closed her eyes. As usual, Colton's caramel brown eyes filled her thoughts. It didn't matter if she was awake or asleep; she'd relived every minute they'd spent together over and over, looking for the clues that she'd missed.

Harper must have dozed off because when she was jolted awake, she felt the tires crunching on gravel. They must have arrived at the Christmas tree farm.

It was late afternoon and the December sun was

almost ready to set. It was so dim in the interior of the car that it was obvious when the car pulled into a well-lit parking lot. Vivian put the car in park and turned off the engine.

"I know you're already awake," her friend said to her back.

"How do you know that?"

"You're so exhausted that you were snoring when you were really sleeping."

"Wonderful. I'll add that to the long list of reasons why Colton is better off without me."

She rolled to her back, stretching, not wanting to get out into the bitter winter wind.

"I have something to tell you, and I need you to stay calm."

"I'm always calm."

"No. You're not. In fact, when you got to my house a few weeks ago, I'd never seen you like that. So upset."

"Yeah, well I'd just had my heart ripped out by a guy I trusted, and then found out the jerk who'd hired me had been secretly taping every second of my life with the intention of ruining my reputation by showing what a fool I was on national television. Gavin Wallace is a complete asshole."

"Well... the asshole is about to open your car door, so try to behave."

When Viv's words sunk in, Harper shot up in her seat so fast she felt lightheaded, although it could also be that she recognized they were sitting in front of the Connecticut mansion that had her feeling like she was about to puke.

The knock on the window next to her startled her. Sure enough, when she turned, it was Gavin leaning down to peer inside the car. The fucker had the gall to smile at her.

A new pain pierced her already damaged heart. Turning, she pinned her best friend with an incredulous glare. Never in a million years would she have expected Vivian to betray her too, delivering her right back into the lion's den.

"Don't look at me like that."

"Like what? Like you're the enemy?"

"Yes," she whispered.

"Too late. Shame on me for being fooled by men I'd never met before, but this? You bringing me here... delivering me right back into my nightmare? How could you, Viv?"

"I trust him."

"Who, Gavin? You've never fucking met him."

"No. Colton."

"You've never met him either."

"You're right. I haven't, but... I can't explain it. I think he's different."

"You are certifiable," Harper accused.

The knocking on the window continued with Gavin trying to coax her out, his voice muffled by the window. "Please, Harper. We need you to come inside for just a few minutes."

She returned her attention to the producer. It was easier to scream at him than her best friend. "Screw you! I'm not so stupid that I'll fall for the same thing twice. I'm not coming in just so you can record more damaging material on me."

"We took all of the hidden cameras out of the entire estate. The only unmanned cameras now are in the garage and security cameras monitoring the perimeter of the house and stables."

"Thanks, but it's a bit too late for me now, isn't it? Don't suppose you erased the hours of damning footage you have on me already, did you?"

He looked conflicted and ended up answering with a noncommittal, "Come inside and we'll talk about the next steps."

"Next steps? Let me see, I think the next steps should be you going to hell and Vivian driving me back to the city."

"If you want to leave, that is totally your prerogative. At least come in and get your paycheck. I didn't know where to mail it."

"That's bullshit. You could have direct deposited it."

He was flustered. "Please, Harper."

A ball of apprehension grew in her tummy at the possibility that Colton might still be on the property. Would she get to see him? Talk to him? Did she even want to?

She looked at her friend for answers. "Colton is here, isn't he? That's why you brought me here?" Her voice quavered as she fought down tears.

Viv nodded, trying to comfort her by brushing her hand. "I talked to him briefly on the phone. I think you should hear him out."

Her mind raced, imagining all the things that could

go wrong to make her feel worse instead of better. "But what if he hurts me even more?"

"Then at least you'll get closure. You're stuck in limbo, kiddo. Go in. Get answers to your questions. Scream at him. Slap his face. Do something. Anything that will help you move on."

Her mind raced for long seconds until she asked, "Will you come with me?"

Viv's smile reassured her. "Of course. If either of them tries to hurt you again, you'll have your wingman. I'll kick 'em in the balls."

Harper couldn't help but giggle at the vision of Gavin and Colton doubled over in excruciating pain.

She must be brain damaged. That was the only explanation for her hand reaching to the door lock and flicking the switch that allowed Gavin to open the door next to her. Bitter winter air blew into the interior.

When he reached his hand in, she slapped it away, unwilling to allow him to help her in any way. She'd only taken a few steps from the car when she stopped dead in her tracks.

The house looked so different.

Gone were the fall decorations, replaced with lit Christmas trees welcoming her from the front porch. The landscape and gardens were decorated with twinkling lights in red, green and white. Most remarkably, the mansion was lit up, peeks of interior holiday decorations could be seen from most of the oversized windows.

"Wow."

Gavin seemed to know where her thoughts had gone.

"The new owner has already been investing in the property."

"New owner? Oh no. I hope the Finnegans aren't going to get evicted."

"Not a chance. They're going to be busier than ever. I can arrange for you to see them tonight if you'd like. They ask about you every day."

"I'd love to see them, but I think it will just make me feel worse. Let's just get my check, and then I should be on my way."

His face fell, but he didn't argue. "If you say so."

Gavin pushed the huge front door open to expose the grand foyer. It had always been a gorgeous home, but tonight, it looked like a she'd fallen into fairytale. The house could be featured in a millionaire home decor magazine. Where before the furnishings had been elegant in their simplicity, the house now looked truly lived in.

With apprehension, she looked up the grand staircase, half expecting the women who'd lived there for the show to be peering down at her, their claws sharpened.

"Please tell me the contestants aren't here any more."

Gavin was behind her, but he didn't answer. She turned, pinning him with an expectant glare.

"They all left just a few hours after you did," he admitted.

"What? That doesn't make any sense. I had to leave so the show could go on without me messing things up."

"No." He paused as if he were picking his words carefully. "You had to leave because Colton refused to let you be used as a pawn to get higher ratings."

She scoffed. "Like I'd get higher ratings than him with Maya and the rest of the girls."

Gavin laughed at her assertion. "Oh, Harper, you and Colton would have been the hottest show of the season."

His use of past tense was not lost on her. "Would have been?" she asked hopefully.

"I think you should ask Colton to explain the rest."

"I thought I was just coming in to get my paycheck."

"You are." He smiled, apologetically. "Colton has it in the dining room. He's waiting for you there."

The tricky bastard. She didn't miss the conspiratorial smiles Gavin and Vivian were sharing.

Could it be true? Colton was just two rooms away? It suddenly hit her. She glanced down at her sorry state of dress. She'd worn clothes to cut down a Christmas tree, never expecting to see Colton King.

Viv must have read her mind. Her friend stepped closer and talked softly, "He only cares about you. He won't care about what you're wearing."

"The least you could have done if you were gonna trick me into coming here is to make me put on a bit more makeup, some lipstick and a bra."

"I'd only kiss the lipstick off, and not having on a bra will save us time later."

It was his voice. So rich and sexy. It sent a jolt through every cell in her body, telling her it was time to wake up and live again.

Her back was to him. She smiled at Viv before retorting, "Still pretty damn sure of yourself I see."

"Are you kidding me? I've never been so nervous in my entire life, and that includes my last at bat in game six of the World Series. We were down one and there were two outs. I was behind on the count and..."

Harper spun around, watching in awe as he nervously rambled on and on. She barely heard what he said, focusing on his non-verbal cues instead.

His anxiety was precious to her. Men like Colton King were always in control. They took what they wanted. The fact that he looked pale, like he might faint at any moment as he looked at her hopefully, humbled her.

She stepped closer, invading his personal space for a change. She lifted her fingers to his lips to shush his skittish rant. He fell silent, looking at her with wide eyes.

"I have questions. Lots of questions. And I need answers. And believe me, Colton James King,"—she paused to smile sweetly, letting him piece together that she had done more research on him while they'd been apart—"if I don't like what I hear, I'm outta here."

He took a calming breath before answering. "I'd expect nothing less," he conceded, looking slightly more relaxed. "We have a meal laid out in the dining room. I know you haven't had supper yet. I'd really like it if you'd stay. We can talk over a dinner someone else prepared for you this time."

"And what about the hidden cameras?" She wanted to hear it from him, not Gavin, that they had been removed.

"Gone. All of them, although..." He looked nervous again. He reached out to place his hands on her two biceps, looking so serious. "I know you aren't going to understand, but I'm still going to ask you to trust me.

There are two cameramen in the dining room waiting for us." When she tried to pull away, he held her tighter. "Please, I know it doesn't make sense to you, but I promise, I'll answer all of your questions, and if at the end of the night you want them to erase the footage, they will. No questions asked. You are in complete control."

"How can that be? I signed that stupid contract, never in a million years thinking I'd end up on even thirty seconds of the show."

"I know that. That's why I bought your contract. Well, to be clear, I bought them all."

"What does that mean, bought them all?"

"It means I control what will be seen, if anything. In essence, I bought out ESPN as the financier of the production."

Gavin grumbled behind her, "The asshole is my boss on the project."

Colton's grin lit up his face. "And don't forget it."

The producer retorted, "I could still press charges you know."

"And I could still fire your ass."

Harper broke in. "Will you two stop it?" she prodded.

Her mind raced at his revelation. She had absolutely no idea how much that would have cost Colt, but it had to be millions.

"Why would you do that?"

He pinned her with a heated stare. "It was the only way I could ensure confidentiality for you—for us. Not to mention, it was the only way I could force the women to leave right away."

"Wait. You spent millions trying to protect your playboy reputation?"

"No, Harper, I spent millions trying to *bury* it. Come sit. I'll tell you everything."

Colton held out his hand like an olive branch. More than anything she wanted to believe what he was saying, but she was so afraid of being taken on another emotional rollercoaster. In the end, she placed her hand in his and let him lead her through the first floor and into the enormous dining room where so many of the meals she'd labored over had been served.

Fresh cut flowers were everywhere. Soft music played. Candles flickered. It was the most romantic scene she'd ever been part of. But there were only two place settings at the head of the table. She glanced around, expecting to find Gavin and Vivian, but found two cameramen in respective corners, a discrete distance away instead.

Her anxiety went through the roof. Fight or flight instincts had her trying to escape to the kitchen, but Colton hugged her, pulling her against his body so he could whisper against her ear. "Just give me a few minutes, and then I promise, I'll send them away, and they'll never come back."

She pulled back far enough so she could look into his expressive eyes. They told a complicated story. She saw desire and lust, but there was so much more there. His anxiety was back in spades, almost overshadowing the tenderness she found most surprising. It made her feel loved, which was crazy since the four-letter-word had never been used by either of them.

Harper allowed herself to be led to the table where

Colton acted the gentleman, pulling out her chair for her to take a seat. Only when she was seated did she notice a small box on the charger plate of the place setting. It looked conspicuously like a jewelry box.

Colton took his seat at the head of the table before reaching to his right to pull an already chilling bottle of champagne from the ice bucket next to him. She tried to calm her fluttering nerves as she watched the handsome man she'd learned she never wanted to live without pour her bubbly, praying she wasn't making an even bigger mistake by trusting him again.

Colt lifted his flute glass when he finished, prompting her to ask her first question. "What are we celebrating?"

He lowered his glass, realizing she wasn't going to just gloss over the hard Q&A session that stood between them and their happily-ever-after.

"For starters, I'm celebrating that you're sitting here with me. I wasn't a hundred percent sure Vivian believed me when we spoke, and even if she did, I was equally uncertain if you'd come back here under any circumstances."

"For the record, she lied to me. I didn't know I was coming here until I woke up in front of the house."

He grinned, unapologetically. "What you're saying, then, is that I owe her one."

"Oh, you owe her way more than that. I almost packed up and drove home to Illinois more than once since I left here. She talked me out of it every single time."

"Why did you stay in New York?"

Wasn't she supposed to be asking all the hard questions? How did he sneak one in?

She found it hard to look him in the eyes as she admitted, "I don't want to go home feeling like a failure. I've been so confused, not understanding what happened. More importantly, I didn't want to always wonder if I'd done all I could before giving up."

"Are you talking about professionally or personally?"

She forced herself to look up at him as she whispered, "Both."

Colt exhaled the breath she suspected he'd been holding while waiting for her answer.

A nervous smile played at the corner of his kissable mouth as he encouraged her. "Then I think it's time you open the box. It should help you answer all of your questions."

As excited as the possibility of opening the box to find an engagement ring made her, she prayed that was not what was inside. It was too fast. While on some subconscious level she felt like she'd known Colton their entire lives, her brain knew the score. He was a playboy who'd never settled down for a year, let alone a lifetime.

He let her sit staring at the box for over a minute before he added a soft plea, "Please, Harper. Trust me."

There it was again. Trust. He wanted it from her, and God did she want to give it, but she'd been hurt so much already. Could she risk more?

She reached out to pick up the small velvet box, pulling it back to hold it in her hand. She glanced up nervously to see he looked like she felt. Scattered.

The tight hinge on the box made it hard to open. She had to work at it, finally prying it open to expose a nice and normal looking key ring. A gold charm of a horse, a second charm of a baseball, and a third of a gold fork dangled from the ring, yet no keys were in sight.

Harper looked up, confused, yet still relieved that he hadn't jumped the gun to jewelry. "I don't understand."

Colton shuffled in his chair to reach into the pocket of his slacks, pulling out three absolutely normal looking keys, placing them in a row on the tablecloth between them. She noticed his fingers were trembling as he picked up the key closest to him and held it out to her. Reflexively, she took the small piece of metal and held it in her lap, not sure if she wanted to ask what it opened.

When her curiosity couldn't stand it anymore, she glanced up to see him smiling as he answered her unasked question. "It's a key to the front door of this house. I bought the entire property, and I want to make it my off-season home. Correction, I'd like to make it our off-season home."

"You bought the house? You did all of this decorating? Oh, please tell me you're going to keep Charlie and Cecelia on. They've lived here almost twenty-five years."

Harper had rambled on, so surprised at his first admission that it took her some time to catch up to what he had really asked her. That was when her tongue got tied as her questions turned more personal.

"You want me to... a key to the house... your off-season..."

Colton's grin was sinful as he corrected her. "No, baby, I said our off-season."

Her hands trembled in her lap, the feel of the key

electrifying her as tears pooled, making the room swim before her.

"Move in with me. Let's get to know each other better before I need to leave for spring training in February."

Harper knew it was a great offer, but his addition of an expiration date certainly put a damper of reality on his offer. Still, it solved the problem of going too fast. Symbolically, she answered him by attaching the key to the key ring.

He was grinning by the time she looked back up at him.

"That was the key for the house." He then picked up the second key and handed it to her, only explaining what it would open after she held it in her hand. "This is a key for my loft in Manhattan. You'll need it when we move back to the city when the season starts."

Tears streamed unchecked down her cheeks as she allowed the relief to wash over her that he hadn't really put an expiration on their relationship before it had really begun. This key represented a longer future together, time to explore what they really had. She couldn't wait another minute, pushing back from the table, and throwing herself into his waiting arms.

Colton navigated her body into his lap as he captured her lips in a heated kiss, hugging her to him so hard she felt squished. Only when she remembered they were being filmed did she try to pull out of the kiss, snuggling close as they held each other silently, enjoying being connected again.

Curiosity eventually returned, prompting her to ask, "So what's the third key for?"

He made sure they could see each other's face as he answered, "It doesn't open anything yet, but it represents the property I'm going to buy you to open your own restaurant. I know it's your dream, and there is no way I'm going to deprive the world of your mushroom ravioli forever."

Not in a million years did she expect those words. It was her dream, but it was too generous. She couldn't accept it.

"Colton..."

He touched his fingers to her lips. "Let's not worry about that one just yet. Selfishly, I'd like to hold off opening the restaurant until after I retire. That way, you can travel with me next season. I won't want to be on the road without you." He paused, choosing his words carefully. "Other than meeting you, that was the best thing about this entire experiment here in Connecticut. It got me really thinking about my future. What comes after baseball? I'm still not sure I have it sorted out, but I do know I'd love to open a restaurant with you. I can lend my name and finances; you bring the talent to make dishes that will have people lining up to eat there. We could make a great team."

She was speechless. It was like a dream come true. He'd mapped out a future that included her standing next to him every step of the way. She couldn't wait to take the key from him and add it to her key ring, symbolizing her commitment to his plan.

They sealed the proposal with a kiss that quickly turned to a groping session as they each held on to the other as if they'd never let go.

When they finally came up for air, Harper only had one final question.

When she could breathe, she prompted him, "So why the cameramen? I thought you canceled the show."

His sexy smile made his caramel-brown eyes twinkle in the candlelight. "The bachelor angle was nixed, yes. Instead, we're doing a mini-series on being a MLB starter for over ten years and how it gets harder to compete against younger players each season while still chasing a world record. The human side of trying to figure out what to do next. After all, all I've ever wanted to do was play baseball."

"Wait. You took the other women out completely?"

"Not a trace of them. Don't worry. I paid them each a fair amount for their time."

Her mind raced. "But... the cameramen are still here."

"That's because like it or not, you are a big part of my story, Harper Gardener. Baseball was my first love, but you are my future. I no longer fear my career ending because, for the first time, I've gotten a glimpse of how many other wonderful things I have ahead of me in my life. I hope you'll be there with me for it all."

Tears of joy streamed down her face as Colton pushed to his feet, Harper scooped in his arms as she snuggled into the crook of his neck. As they passed through the kitchen, out of the corner of her eye, she saw Cecelia, tears streaming down her face as she smiled at the couple.

They were halfway up the back steps when she found her voice. "Where are we going? I thought we were going to have dinner?"

Colton chuckled. "I'm pretty sure Cecelia will

understand that we're going to need room service tonight. In fact, I'm not planning to leave our room for a few days."

Harper hugged him tighter, loving his idea until she remembered to add. "That sounds perfect, just so long as there are no more cameras there."

"No cameras. Only sex toys. I stocked up. I can't wait to watch you pleasure yourself again like that first night. That was the hottest damn thing I'd ever seen in my life."

They'd entered a huge master bedroom where a king sized bed waited for them. Colton dropped her into the center and then dove on top of her.

That's when it hit her. This bed. His bed. It was now theirs. This gorgeous house she'd admired while working there, was her new home. And the man who was busy sucking her nipple into his mouth, he was her future. The king in her fairytale.

Her American royalty.

Keep Reading! There's more :)

BONUS SCENES: CHRISTMAS MORNING

"Time to rise and shine, sleepyhead. I'm starving."

Harper groaned, rolled onto her tummy, and pulled the luxurious bedding of their king-sized bed over her head to block out the sun shining through the window facing the sunrise. She didn't know the time, but she knew it was too early.

"I don't wanna get up yet. I'm too tired."

The rich, masculine chuckle that preceded the good-natured swat to her ass did things to her girly parts. Colton had kept her up half the night exploring one sexual adventure after another. The fact that every part of her body was sore was testament to her lover's dedication to living up to his pledge to never let her forget how much she was loved.

"It's Christmas morning. Don't you want your gifts?" he prodded. His voice was muffled, barely audible with her head burrowed under the pillow.

"No more gifts," she protested.

Living with him for the last two weeks had been like receiving one big huge gift after another. He'd already bought her a closet of new clothes, a half dozen new pairs of shoes and a suitcase full of beach gear for their planned trip to the Caribbean right after the new year. And that didn't even include the outrageous amount of money he had been spending on renovations, furniture and decorations to turn the mansion into their home. If he didn't spend another dime on her for the next year, he still would have already spent too much.

Colton pulled the covers back, peeling the pillow away from her head and exposing her to the stream of sunlight again. "I thought you told me you were a morning person. I think you lied to me," he teased.

Only then did the smell of coffee and pancakes register with Harper and her tummy growled. Deciding coffee was a welcome gift after all, she propped herself up on her elbows, her long hair tangled in a rat's nest. She knew she must look like a hot mess, but they'd been pretty much holed up in the master bedroom for weeks, so there was nothing Colton King had not seen.

And yet, thankfully, he still wants me.

She dished banter back as she reached for the coffee mug on the tray next to her. "I explained this to you. I am a morning person when I actually get to sleep. When someone keeps me up half the night, I'm afraid I might want to sleep in."

He leaned down to kiss her naked shoulder as she took a sip of java, trying not to spill coffee on the already sex-soiled sheets.

"Is that a complaint? You didn't seem to mind around three this morning." His lips trailed down her back, lightly spreading heat with his touch.

"Em...no. Definitely not a complaint. More like an observation." The coffee sloshed over the side of the big mug as Harper shivered from the affects of his nibbles.

Colton pulled back abruptly, making her miss the warmth of his touch.

"Well, today is special. It's Christmas. I think I'm more excited for you to open your gifts than I am to get my own." Before she could protest the additional presents, he added, "Your first gift from me is breakfast in bed. Time to turn around and sit up."

The heavenly aroma of pancakes and maple syrup forced Harper into motion. They'd eaten many meals in the bedroom and had a routine. Colton lifted the oversized bamboo bed tray while Harper negotiated herself to sitting with her back against the slatted headboard. Only after he placed the tray across her lap did he pick up a pillow, silently holding it until she leaned forward and then he fluffed it at her back, making things more comfortable for her.

Harper took in the full tray of goodies. He'd outdone himself. A large stack of pancakes was just the beginning. He'd fried bacon, sausage and hash browns. There were two hard-boiled eggs and even a bowl of fresh berries with whipped cream on top. Finishing things off was a pot of coffee, two mugs and a fruit smoothie to drink.

"This better be for both of us," she quipped, grabbing a slice of bacon first.

He grinned down at her, and she didn't miss his attention moving from her eyes to her naked breasts. "I nibbled while I cooked, but I was hoping to nibble a bit up here too."

She was about to tease him about his nibbles when it hit her. "Wait. You cooked? Don't you mean while you waited for Cecelia to cook?"

The handsome man with the scruffy morning beard and messed up hair grinned as he settled on the bed facing her. "I resent that incredulous tone, young lady. I gave Cecelia and Charlie the day off, of course. I know I can't cook like you, but I can manage a breakfast."

"Wow, I'm impressed. Is there anything you can't do?" It was an honest question. He was perfect. As she sipped her hot coffee, she noticed he'd even added a touch of French vanilla creamer to her cup like she preferred.

"Oh, I'm sure there's plenty, but right now I want to focus on the things I can do." He grinned mischievously as he reached with his index finger to scoop up a big dollop of whipped cream from on top of the berries. She recognized the sexual glaze in his eyes as he reached to cover first her right and then left nipple in the white cream.

It was cold. She squealed, reaching to remove the offending chill. But he was too fast for her, grabbing both her wrists and lifting her hands above her head.

"Oh no you don't. Hold onto the head rail and don't let go until I tell you," he ordered.

"But it's freezing!" She could feel her nipples peaking under the fluffy covering.

"I'll take care of warming you up. Don't worry."

Harper bucked her ass up off the bed when he lunged forward, sucking her right nipple into his warm mouth, nipping down hard enough that it startled her. She almost tipped over the tray of food in the process.

"Whoa, there, baby. Hold still while I start my breakfast." He looked up from her breast, whipped cream covering his lips. She could feel her core contracting as he slowly used the tip of his tongue to lick it off his lips before grinning.

He is the sexiest man alive and he's all mine.

He first lifted the tray away, leaving it on the bed before pulling the covers down and grabbing her legs. She squealed as he pulled her down to lay flat before straddling her knees. Once he had exactly as he wanted, he returned his attention to his breakfast. Picking up several raspberries and blackberries, he placed them in a line from the valley of her perky breasts to her belly button.

Starting at her waist, he seductively sucked one berry into his mouth after the other until he'd eaten them all. He finished his appetizer at her left tit–licking and sucking the whipped cream and finally nipping at her nipple until it protruded obscenely.

When he leaned up, he grinned, proud of himself for her obvious humping, hoping he might repeat his attention below her waist as well.

It wasn't meant to be. He stood, moving the tray back over her lap. But when Harper let go of the headboard, he reached to lightly slap her taut nipple as punishment.

"I didn't say you could let go, did I?"

That tone. She fucking loved that tone he used in their bedroom. The one that told her he was in charge, and here... behind the double doors of their bedroom... she'd discovered that was just fine with her.

"No, sir," she replied, knowing first hand the effect those words had on his magnificent cock. The salutation was like a magic potion. As she glanced down at his lap, she could see his rod straining against his sleep pants and smiled.

"Christ, we may never make it downstairs for the rest of the presents if you keep calling me sir."

Harper grinned. "That's fine by me. I don't need any more gifts. You've already given me too much."

He cut a bite of pancake, poked it with a fork and held it up to her mouth. "You're gonna have to get used to it, Harper," he answered seriously. "We have money."

"No, you have money."

"Enough. I don't want to talk about this today. It's Christmas. Please, let me spoil you. We can argue about money again tomorrow, okay?" He pinned her with a serious glare that told her he wasn't going to back down.

She didn't want to ruin their first Christmas together by arguing either.

"Okay. You'll get a one day reprieve, but I'm serious. I don't need you to spend money on me to know you love me."

He shoveled another bite of pancakes in his mouth before he answered, "And that is just one of the many things I love about you, baby. Now let's get you fed."

Nervous excitement danced in his eyes as he fed her from the food on the tray, occasionally directing bites to himself. He had a goofy grin by the time he finished feeding her. It reminded her of a kid on Christmas morning.

His excitement was contagious. She couldn't wait to see his face when she gave him the gifts she'd picked out for him. It hadn't been easy to come up with presents for a man who had everything he needed and the money to buy anything he wanted. She'd put a lot of thought into her presents though.

"Okay, you can let go of the bed now. Go in and brush your teeth and throw on some comfy clothes. I'll have your next gift waiting for you by the time you get out of the bathroom."

"My next? Why does it sound like there are more even after the next one?"

"I thought we agreed not to talk money today?" he warned.

She hesitated before snapping, "Fine. I'll go along for a bit, but if you filled another closet, we are going to have some problems."

"Nope. No more filling of closets." He paused before adding, "At least not until we get back to New York."

"Oh goodie. That's at least a few weeks," she added dryly.

He swatted her naked ass as she finally got out of bed, and she hustled to the bathroom with its heated floors. There was even a small heater in the wall that she loved on a cold Connecticut December morning.

By the time she finished her morning routine and returned to their bedroom dressed in comfortable yoga pants and one of Colton's oversized Yankee's sweatshirts, all evidence of breakfast was gone and a large, wrapped box sat on the bed in the place she had just vacated. The present was elegantly wrapped with blue and silver paper and a shiny silver bow on top. It was hard for her to tell which was brighter, that bow or the joy on Colton's face.

"I can't wait to see if you like it."

It still surprised her that there were times when she sensed an insecurity in her celebrity, larger-than-life boyfriend. He was confident in so many things, but there were times, like this morning, when she was reminded that, while he may be a very experienced man-whore by most women's standards, he was very new to the whole relationship thing. Harper loved that he had never been in a relationship like the one they now shared. Serious. Committed.

In love, not lust.

She let his excitement infect her. "I'm sure I'll love it. Should I open it here, or should we take it downstairs? I put my gifts for you under the big tree already."

"Oh, I have other things for you down there too, but I wanted you to open this one here first."

She gave him the stink eye at finding out there were even more presents downstairs, but she let it go. She wasn't going to ruin his excitement.

Just as she was about to lift the wrapped top off the box, it jiggled. The box muffled a gruff growl.

"It's alive!" she said, stepping back reflexively.

Colton chuckled. "It's okay. He's not going to hurt you."

"He? You promise?"

"I promise. Although, he might do a little damage to the house." He grinned her way. "You'll see. Open it."

Harper lifted one corner, intending to peek inside slowly, but the second the lid left the box, an adorable puppy jumped up, landing on the side of the box and tipping it over. Before she could even react, the little tyke was running around, sniffing at their bedding and acting like he was about to pee in the middle of the bed.

Colton lunged to catch him just as he jumped off the bed and took off running. Harper couldn't stop herself from laughing as she watched the ten pound fluff ball get the best of the star athlete in the room.

"Come back here, you little shit!" he cursed.

Non-pulsed, the pup made the rounds in the room until finally approaching Harper. She squatted to the floor, holding out her hands, and the puppy ran right into her arms. The second the wiggle-butt was in her grasp, he settled down, snuggling into her embrace as she stood. The second their eyes met, Harper fell in love for the second time that month.

"I don't know why you feel the need to yell at the little guy. He seems happy to me." She stroked the soft, caramel colored fur.

Despite the aggravation, Colton still grinned as he watched them bond.

She hadn't even considered that he might get them a pet, so she was shocked by this gift. She had questions.

"What kind of puppy is he?"

"He's a Havenese."

"How old is he?"

"I got him from a breeder. He just turned four months old."

"Oh, you little baby. I bet you miss your mama, don't you?"

"He stayed with Cecelia and Charlie last night. They said he cried most of the night." Harper looked up in time to see the flash of fear in his eyes. "I hope I didn't make a big mistake. What the hell do I know about taking care of a baby?"

Harper smiled reassuringly as she walked across the room towards him. Only when he was close enough to reach out and pet the puppy did she add, "You'll do fine. In fact, I think practicing on a puppy is a good idea, don't you?"

His eyes grew large. "What? You aren't... I mean... we're not going to..."

She reached up to place her fingers over his lips to stop his insecure rambling. "No, Colt. I'm not pregnant. I'm just making an observation that you will be wonderful with a puppy."

"Oh. Well, okay."

"What's his name?"

"I didn't name him, yet. I thought you should have the honors."

Already bored with standing still, the furball was wiggling in her arms to be free. Harper squeezed him to her, lifting his face to hers. "What do you say, little guy? What should we name you?"

"I'm not sure he's going to answer, baby. I didn't lug everything upstairs, but there is a whole box of supplies we'll need for him down in the back entryway. A doggie bed, leash, bowl, puppy food, treats... you name it. I'm not sure, but I think the lady at the pet store fleeced me a little bit."

Harper grinned as the pup leaned in and licked her cheek. "I think he likes me."

Colton hugged her from behind, leaning in to talk softly against her ear. "Of course he likes you. You're perfect." His hands roamed over her body. With the puppy in her arms, she wasn't able to fend him off. Then again she didn't really want to.

"I hope he gets along with Wrigley. He's so much smaller than a German Shepherd."

Colton reassured her, "They got along great, according to Cecelia."

That's when it hit her. She turned so she could see Colton. "I think I know what we should name him."

"What's that?"

"Well, we already have a Wrigley. I think we should name him Yankee for the stadium you've spent so much time playing in."

He didn't answer her, but she knew from the sparkle in his eyes that he liked the idea. Still, he argued against it. "It's your puppy. You don't have to name him for my career."

"Will you stop it? It's a cute name, especially with Wrigley. And then our next puppy we can name Fenway, and maybe the one after Shea."

Colt chuckled. "I love it. Really. It's perfect."

"I'm a little worried I'm not going to like leaving him home when we go on the road later this spring."

"But that's the great thing. I got a small breed so he can travel with us." He paused, looking like he was debating if he wanted to continue. She waited him out until he added, "You're going to have a lot of downtime, and I don't want you getting lonely in hotels. I'll have to go to the stadium for warm up way before you. And I'll have team meetings and practices. I'm worried you might get bored, and so I thought you'd enjoy having a travel companion."

She was floored. She already loved the puppy, but understanding his reason for buying him for her made her love the gift even more. "Oh, Colton. That's so thoughtful." She sat Yankee down on the carpet so she could be free to properly thank Colton for the awesome gift. She rushed forward, pulling him into a tight hug.

He crushed her with a heated kiss that was just getting interesting when a pungent odor invaded. They pulled out of the kiss in time to see Yankee finishing depositing his own unwanted gift in the middle of the room, right on the cream carpet.

"I'm beginning to think I might have made a mistake."

Harper rushed to scoop up the untrained member of their family. "Too late now. I already love him."

Colton grumbled. "Great. The carpets will never be the same."

Colton finished putting the dirty dishes in the dishwasher and then wiped off the counter. Part of serving Harper breakfast in bed was doing clean up too.

He took a minute to stop and admire the upscale kitchen. It was modern and spacious--sporting industrial-sized appliances that he hoped would be his chef's pride and joy. Sometimes he had to pinch himself to remember that this was now his home. And more importantly, that he had found the one special person he wanted to share it all with.

He felt like the luckiest bastard on the planet.

Colton may have joked with Harper that he regretted buying her the puppy, but seeing the light sparkling in her eyes as she played with the little shit solidified that he'd made the right decision.

The last few weeks living with Harper had been the best of his life, spending every minute he could with her. He could honestly say he loved her more every single day as they got to know each other better.

But he knew something Harper didn't.

They were in a cocoon. Sheltered. They wouldn't always have it as easy as they did hiding out in their new mansion in Connecticut--away from the press and the paparazzi that dogged him wherever he went. Away from reporters looking for an interesting angle on a story, not caring if they decimated his private life in the process.

The minute the press found out one of the country's most eligible bachelors was officially off the market, the sharks would start to circle. It hadn't been too bad for the first few years of his career, but when he'd been chosen as

People Magazine's Sexiest Man Alive three years ago, things had escalated. Being crowned sports royalty by the media had torn down the last hint of a wall between his public and private life. The press had turned into piranhas. They would chew up and spit out Harper if he wasn't careful.

But he had a plan.

He'd been at this fame thing long enough to know how the game was played, and this time, he was going on offense. He would protect Harper from as much as he could, but if in the end, the public life got too hard on their relationship, he was prepared to walk away from the game he loved, with or without the world record he was chasing.

"I got the poop all cleaned up. The good thing about him being a small dog is he makes small poop." Harper's cheery voice arriving from the back stairwell broke him out of his brooding.

He turned to see her carrying their newest member of the household. "That's comforting. Training him to go outside should be fun. Let's just hope he's a fast learner."

Colt grabbed the two mugs of fresh, hot coffee he'd brewed from the counter. "You ready to head into the great room and open the rest of your gifts?"

Little did Harper know her best gift wasn't in the great room. In fact, it wasn't even in the house. A niggle of doubt rattled in his head, but he pushed it down. He knew she was going to be angry at the last gift, but he didn't care. It was something she needed, whether she would admit it or not.

The two-story great room sported an equally tall

Christmas tree. They had had so much fun the week before hiking out into the woods on their property, looking for the perfect tree. They'd spotted this one and had known right away it was the one. What they hadn't realized was how much effort it would take getting such a huge tree back to the house. He'd spent damn near a fortune on the decorations and it still looked a bit empty.

Harper led him to the couch facing the fireplace and tree. "You take a seat and hold Yankee. I'll bring our gifts over from under the tree."

Apparently the littlest member of the household had already tuckered himself out because the second Harper placed him in Colt's lap, the furball curled up and nodded off to sleep.

Harper laid a pile of wrapped gifts on the couch next to him before taking a seat on the other side of the pile.

"Do you have any idea how hard you are to buy for?" she observed nervously.

"That's not true. I'm not picky."

"Maybe not, but you have everything you need already."

"I don't know," he teased. "I could use about ninety-four more double base hits."

Harper grinned as she retorted, "They were fresh out of those when I went shopping."

Colt reached his hand out to squeeze her shoulder reassuringly. "Stop worrying. I'm sure I'll love whatever you got me."

"I hope so. They seemed like a good idea when I was deciding, but now I'm not so sure." She lifted one of the wrapped boxes between them and handed it to him. "Open this one first."

The box wasn't very heavy. He took his time pulling the ribbon off the package and tearing the paper off, wanting to make the moment last. How long had it been since he'd had a special Christmas morning like this? His parents and grandparents were gone. He was an only child. Traveling non-stop, he'd lost touch with his aunts, uncles and cousins.

Colt lifted the lid from the box to find tissue paper hiding the treasure inside. When he uncovered the gift, he found what looked like a handmade scrapbook inside. Harper helped him by taking the box so he could hold the book above the sleeping puppy.

The first page held an 8x10 worn photo of what looked like an extended family standing at the altar of a church, surrounding a too-young bride and groom.

He was confused.

"It's my whole family at my cousin Heather's wedding two years ago. They just had their first baby in October." He could hear vulnerability in her voice as she continued, "Turn the page."

On the next two pages was an older wedding picture along with about a half-dozen photos of the same couple as they'd aged together.

"Those are my parents, Bill and Jennifer. They've been married for thirty-five years now."

He turned the page.

"That's my brother Hayden. He's seven years older than me. He farms with my dad and my uncle. And that's his wife, Margie, and their three boys." She got quiet so he looked up as she added, "I know we are a big crew. It can be a little overwhelming meeting everyone. I thought it might make it easier if you could see pictures and learn their names ahead of time."

His heart raced as he started to understand the meaning behind her gift. He'd never dated anyone long enough to meet their family. He was usually long gone before things got serious enough to meet the folks.

Harper was making a statement. He wasn't just dating her. If he had his way, he would be becoming a member of the family on the pages he held.

As he got deeper into the book, page after page was filled with dozens of people and places that were important to Harper, which by default now meant they were important to him.

His voice was thick with emotion when he finally spoke. "I love it. It means so much to know you did this so I could feel like part of the family when I meet them."

"You don't think it's stupid?"

"Baby, like you said. I have what I need already. This gift is so much more than just buying something fancy. It's personal and makes me feel part of a family again, something that's been missing in my life for a long time."

He sensed her relaxing, relieved he'd liked her odd, yet thoughtful, gift.

He lifted the largest box between them and held it out to her. "Your turn to open a present." He set it down closer to her where she could reach the paper.

"You already gave me Yankee. That was more than enough," she protested.

"Listen, you made me stop buying you things for no

occasion. You can't make me stop giving for Christmas too. It would be very Scrooge-like to refuse my gift."

Harper eyed him skeptically. "Seriously. You've spent enough..."

He reached out to hold two fingers at her lips to shush her. "Stop. I can afford it, and I love buying things for you. Please, just unwrap it and see what you think."

"Fine. But only because it's Christmas. You need to get this spending under control."

Colton couldn't help but laugh out loud.

"What's so damn funny?" she prodded, clearly aggravated.

"I've never had a woman tell me to stop spending money on her. Usually, it's the other way around with me playing the role of the checkbook in the relationship."

"Well, I don't give a damn about your checkbook, and you'd better get used to it," Harper asserted.

He appreciated she wasn't with him for his money, but he needed to get through to her. "Well, I have money, and I want to spend some of it on you and you'd better get used to that." He paused before adding, "Just open the damn present, will you? You're taking the fun out of this."

"Fine," she huffed, finally moving the package closer to her. It was fascinating to watch her methodically take off the ribbons and bows first followed by removing the paper in one big section before folding it up.

"Eh, baby?"

"Yes."

"What exactly do you plan on doing with the used paper?" he questioned.

"Save it, of course. It's perfectly good paper."

"You do realize we can buy more next year."

She looked at him as if he were daft. "Of course, but why throw away perfectly good paper?"

He let it go.

He'd had the store place both items together in one brown box to throw her off. They'd taped it pretty good as was proven when she struggled to get the line of packing tape off the top of the box. He held his breath when she succeeded, waiting for her to open the present and lose her shit on him.

He knew the second she saw the first item. She didn't even pick it up, but instead returned to glaring at him.

"What?" he asked innocently. "You need this."

"I do not need anything from Apple."

"I beg to differ. Come on, let's take a look."

She reached in and pulled out the iPad box. She held it close, looking down at the box until she finally glanced up. That was when he saw the excitement in her eyes.

"Okay, I take it back. I think I'm going to love this gift. Vivian has one, and I used to borrow it. Thank you so much, Colton," she gushed.

Harper rushed to open the box and take the newest model out to turn it around in her hands admiringly.

Colton shared his main reason for the purchase. "You're going to have a lot of downtime this next year on the road. Time waiting in airports and hotels. Hell, even at stadiums. I figured this would be something you could take along to read, watch movies, surf or listen to music."

"Or play Candy Crush." She grinned, hugging the iPad to her chest lovingly.

He chuckled. "I actually prefer Angry Birds, but you can play whatever you want, baby."

She moved closer on the couch so she could lean in and give him a tight hug over the remaining presents. Yankee, who had been enjoying sleeping in his lap, wiggled awake.

Harper picked up the last present on the couch to hand to him. After he took the gift, he let her know she wasn't yet done. "The iPad wasn't the only thing in the box. Keep digging."

"What? No way!"

"Harper..." he growled in warning.

She wisely stopped complaining and started pulling the packing tissue paper out until she'd dug down to the second gift.

"Beats! Oh this will be awesome for listening to music." She excitedly worked to open the box.

"I got you the wireless ones. You'll need these with the iPad."

"Oh, Colton, I love them. Thank you so much." He watched as her excitement dimmed and a worried frown replaced her glee.

"What's wrong?"

She hesitated before admitting, "I got you stupid things compared to your gifts. You must be so disappointed."

He moved closer to her on the couch, disturbing the puppy again in the process. "Harper, just you being here with me is gift enough. If we hadn't met, I'd be golfing today down in Florida with a bunch of old farts who don't have anywhere better to be either."

"Golfing? On Christmas morning?"

"That's what I've done for the last two years. I don't have a family and while I have lots of friends and associates who regularly invite me over, the few times I went to someone's house to celebrate with them made me feel worse. I was like a fifth wheel, interrupting their family time. It was easier to just head down to Florida and golf with a bunch of other guys in the same boat as me."

"Oh, Colton, that sounds terrible."

"It wasn't so bad, but..."

"What?"

He hesitated, feeling vulnerable, but refusing to tell her anything but the truth. "But now that I know how special it is to share Christmas with someone I love, I can't possibly go back to enjoying golfing for the holiday ever again."

His meaning hung in the air between them, raw and sincere.

Her warm hand cupping his scruffy cheek felt good. "You'll never have to worry about that again if I have anything to say about it, Colton."

He covered her hand with his, squeezing. "Then that's the best Christmas present you can give me, Harper. You being here with me is the gift I didn't even know I wanted... no, *needed*. But now that you are part of my life, I can't even imagine going back to the way things were."

Her reassuring smile eased his unusual anxiety. She reached down to hand him a pile of gifts attached together with a thick ribbon. "You have a few more things to open."

He started with the smallest square box on top.

Unlike Harper, he ripped the paper quickly away to find a Christmas ornament box. It was no ordinary ornament, however. It was hand-blown glass in gold, silver and white in the form of a picture frame. He opened the box to pull out the ornament to find a photo of Harper and him smiling loving at each other with the words, 'Our First Christmas Together' above them. His heart constricted with emotion.

"Where did you get this photo? It's really good," he observed.

"At least Gavin was good for something. He helped me arrange to get some candids of us from the camera crew."

"Well, it's perfect."

Harper shared, "I have always enjoyed collecting ornaments when I travel. I figured we could buy special ornaments together while we are on the road next year."

He was touched. "I love that idea. Souvenirs as we make new memories together."

Her eyes twinkled as she knew he understood her plan. "Keep unwrapping."

The next box held two Christmas stockings, one with *Colton* and the other with *Harper* embroidered on the top. He barely got them open when she snatched them from his hands, and jumped up, rushing to the fireplace to attach them to already waiting hooks on the mantel.

"We need stockings for Christmas morning."

She spun around when she completed hanging them, excitement on her eyes. He couldn't resist saying the first thing that came to his mind.

"Actually, they look a little lonely up there on the

huge mantel." He paused, watching her reaction carefully. "I can't wait until we can add a few more to the line... like Yankee and... our kids one day."

They hadn't talked children yet, but knowing Harper had a pretty big extended family, he was hopeful he hadn't just freaked her out. He held his breath waiting for her reaction.

Her response came in the form of an adorable blush that spread quickly down her neck. She stammered a reply that told him how flustered she was. "Kids? As in children?"

"Yes, baby. That's what kids usually means, unless you want to get goats."

"Don't make a joke when we're talking about something so serious. We barely know each other."

"Bullshit. We're living together, buying pets and furniture together and about to travel the country together. I don't think talking about kids is that out of line."

"I didn't say it was out of line. I mean... it's just..." Her voice trailed off.

He set the sleeping puppy onto the couch and got up to go to her. He didn't waste time on words. He went straight for the panty-wetting open-mouthed kiss that stopped her nervous rant.

When the kiss ended, he stayed close, their foreheads touching as he looked down into her teary eyes. "I didn't mean to rush you. A few months ago, I never would have thought the topic would be important to me, but now that I've met you, I've thought of it a lot. I'm not going to be happy until I can hold at least one adorable little girl who looks just like her mama."

"Colton, you say the most romantic things."

They enjoyed holding each other for a few moments before Harper pulled away. "You have a few more things to open."

Yankee settled into Harper's lap as he reached for the last box between them. Like the first box he'd opened, it looked like a picture album, but this time, the object of the photos were all himself with Harper. It was a diary of their short time together, with candid photos of them together riding out on the horses, picnicking along the banks of the pond on the property and even talking together their first night in the huge garage.

"I figured something good could come out of all of those hours of footage. The production crew was able to find the best frames of us together."

When he got to the final pages, there were photos of the night she'd returned to the estate. Them, in their dining room as she'd opened the keys that represented so much. The camera crew had done a great job capturing their emotions and the photos moved him.

"I love it, Harper. Truly, your gifts were so thoughtful. Thank you."

"Well, I love my gifts too. I know that you got me Yankee and my iPad to help ease me into the changes that are coming this year when you go back to work."

"I'm just grateful you're going to be with me. It gets lonely on the road."

"Not anymore, it won't be." She reached for the iPad. "Time to play with my new toy," she gushed.

"Not quite yet. You still have one more gift coming."

Her eyes narrowed, ready to argue, but she wisely didn't pick a fight. "I don't see any more gifts under the tree."

"That's because it isn't there." He hesitated nervously before adding, "It was too big to fit."

"Colton," she warned.

"Harper," he returned adding, "You're going to complain at first, but when you stop and think about it, you'll know I was right. I got you something that you really need."

"We'll see about that. Exactly where do I go to find my present?"

"Just outside the front door. Let's go."

He pulled her to her feet, letting her carry the little furball that was wiggling in her arms and fighting to get down and run.

Colton paused before opening the door, turning to her and asking, "I have one favor to ask. Before you lose your shit on me, please know that I did this because I want to keep you safe. You are important to me."

He saw the confusion on her face at his words so he prompted her, "Just open the door. You'll see."

He'd peeked out to make sure all was ready before they'd sat down to open presents. Now, seeing how she'd protested at her smaller gifts, he knew they were about to have an argument, but he'd been honest with her. It was important to him to keep her safe.

Harper opened the door and stepped out onto the front porch. There was one long second of silence and then a blood-curdling scream from the woman next to him. The racket startled Yankee and he wiggled out of Harper's arms. It was a bad sign that she was too distracted to even notice her puppy was now loose and on the run outside.

As soon as her scream died down, he put his arm around her waist and leaned in close. "Take a deep breath. Before you get too pissed, they aren't all for you. I didn't know what you'd want so I had them bring out some choices. You pick the one you want. They're coming back out tomorrow to pick up the ones you don't choose."

"But... they are cars. Real vehicles."

He chuckled. "Yes. Very observant. Actually, one is an SUV.

Three vehicles were parked facing the house, on display in a semi-circle, each with a huge red bow on the hood along with a big number 1, 2 and 3 to identify them.

"So you get to pick which is your favorite. Number one is a nice steady Volkswagen sedan. I picked that one because they have some of the best safety records in the market. Number two is a Lexus GX460, a very good multi-purpose vehicle. Number three I was less sure of, but the dealer talked me into throwing it into the mix in case you wanted more of a sports car. It's a BMW M6 convertible."

It was as if she hadn't heard him as she repeated, "But they are real cars."

"Come on, let's chase down Yankee first and then you can sit in each one. Maybe take them for a drive before you decide which one you want to keep. I've worked with this car broker for years. He said if you want a different color or anything, to just let him know. He'll track down whatever you want."

"Are you nuts? I'm not keeping any of them! I already have a car," she protested as he started to pull her towards the front steps.

"No, you have a broken down, untrustworthy heap that I don't want you out driving in. It made me nervous last week when you were gone shopping. I didn't know if you'd make it back or not with your Honda."

"But I like my Honda. I don't need anything new."

"Yes, Harper, you do. If you really love Hondas, we could send all of three back and go looking for a Honda together next week."

He somehow succeeded in getting her to the driver's side of the sedan just as Yankee arrived there. "Hey, look. It looks like Yankee wants to give each of them a try with you. Go on. Open it up."

In a trance, Harper did as she was told, opening the door and slowly lowering herself into the driver's seat of the Passat. She slowly looked around the space, yet acted afraid to touch anything.

"You want to take it for a test drive? He said he'd leave the keys in it."

"No. I told you. I'm not keeping them."

Discouraged, Colt helped her out of the first car and moved to the next one in line, the luxury SUV. This one, Harper resisted even sitting in.

"How much do these cost? They all look brand new."

"It doesn't matter how much they cost and, yes, they are new."

"I have never bought a new vehicle. My dad says to buy used. They are a better value."

"Maybe, but I don't care about that. I don't want you driving around in someone else's castoff. Who the hell knows why they sold it. I don't want you to have any used car troubles."

"But..."

He put his foot down. "Sit in the Lexus, Harper. Try it out."

Unlike the sedan, once seated, she started to explore in the SUV, turning on the engine and playing with the knobs and accessories.

"Are these heated seats?" she asked quietly.

"Looks like it. I like the navigation system on this one, too. And the Bluetooth surround sound entertainment system. It looks like it even has the rear camera for backup help and the tow package if we ever wanted to pull anything behind."

"What in the world would we ever pull behind?"

"Maybe a horse trailer? I assume we're going to keep the stables full for Charlie."

He scored points with that answer. He saw the excitement in her eyes at the thought of getting more horses for their large stable.

After letting her sit in the SUV for a few minutes, he asked, "You want to move to the next one?"

When she didn't answer, he let her continue to silently fiddle with all of the nooks and crannies of the interior. He was getting chilled standing in the open driver's side door, so he and Yankee stepped back and closed the door. He walked around to get into the passenger side.

The warm bucket seat felt good on his cold ass. Yankee wiggled around, trying to get away from him so he set the pup down in the back seat, praying he didn't pee on the leather seats.

"Let's take her for a spin, shall we?" he suggested.

"Oh no. We shouldn't. I don't need a new car," she protested again, although he noted with much less force than before.

Colt leaned across the center console, thrusting his left hand into Harper's long and messy hair, pulling her around to face him.

"Harper Gardener, we are replacing your Honda. If you don't like these choices, we can go shopping together to find you something you like better, but I'm putting my foot down. You're getting something more dependable than what you have."

She tried to interrupt, but he kissed her quiet. When they pulled out of their kiss, he continued on, "And before you complain about the price, I need you to understand something. I make enough money by playing just one game to buy all three of these cars. And to top it off, as soon as Van finds out I bought you a Lexus, he'll be on the phone with the Lexus marketing department to make a deal. They'll pay me millions for an endorsement. Just one advertising campaign will pay for a whole truckload of these. So please, stop worrying about the money."

Her eyes widened at his explanation of how much money celebrities like him can make if they really worked their connections. As an athlete, his talents had a shelf life. He used to worry about what would come next after he was forced out of baseball, the only career he'd known and that he loved.

But he was no longer worried about that now that he had Harper by his side.

"So what do you say? I can tell you like this one a lot," he prompted.

She pulled out of their embrace and looked around the interior with tears of excitement in her eyes. When she finally looked back at him, she had that stubborn glint in her eyes that he'd come to love about her.

"I do love this one, I admit it. But I have one more favor to ask if we are really going to keep it."

He hadn't expected her to give in so easily. "Okay, name it."

"I'd like to drive to see my family next week instead of flying. They're pretty far away from the airport, and we were going to be stuck at the farm without transportation which had me a bit worried."

"So. You want to take our first road trip?"

"Yep. And with Yankee being so young, it will be easier on him if we can stop for potty breaks. And..."

Her voice trailed off.

"And what?"

Harper looked uncomfortable as she finally answered him. "I admit, I'm sort of dreading going out in public with you for the first time. Once we get to the airport, I'm sure you'll be recognized, and it'll only be a matter of time before the paparazzi track us down. I know we can't hide forever, but if it's all the same to you, I'd like to keep the King of Baseball all to myself for a bit longer."

Colton's heart melted at the love he saw shining in her eyes. "Baby, I'm all yours. You want to celebrate by taking a drive?"

She shook her head and replied, "I'd rather celebrate inside. Upstairs. In bed."

"Sounds like the perfect Christmas celebration to me. Let's go."

GET A FREE BLACK LIGHT BOOK

Did you enjoy Livia Grant's storytelling? She has so many books available and there's a lot more sexy fun to be had! If you haven't found her ***Black Light*** series yet, what are you waiting for?

Get started with a FREE copy of ***Black Light: Rocked*** today. Your fun doesn't need to end yet! It is a standalone with no cliffhanger!

BLACK COLLAR PRESS

About the Author

USA Today bestselling author Livia Grant lives in Chicago with her husband and furry rescue dog named Max. She is fortunate to have been able to travel extensively and as much as she loves to visit places around the globe, the Midwest and its changing seasons will always be home. Livia's readers appreciate her riveting stories filled with deep, character driven plots, often spiced with elements of BDSM.

Connect with Livia!
www.liviagrant.com
lb.grant@yahoo.com
New Release Newsletter

ALSO BY LIVIA GRANT

Dark Pen Series

Devil's Contract - With Alta Hensley

Black Light Series

Infamous Love, A Black Light Prequel

Black Light: Rocked

Black Light: Valentine Roulette

Black Light: Rescued

Black Light: Roulette Redux

Complicated Love

Black Light: Celebrity Roulette

Black Light: Purged

Black Light: Scandalized

Black Light: Roulette War

Black Light: The Beginning

Black Light: Roulette Rematch

Black Light: Gamble - coming 2022

Black Light: Rolled - coming 2022

Punishment Pit Series

Wanting it All

Securing it All

Having it All

Balancing it All

Defending it All

Protecting it All

Expecting it All

Celebrating it All

Deceiving it All - Coming 2022

Stand Alone Books

Blessed Betrayal

Royalty, American Style

Alpha's Capture (as Livia Bourne)

Blinding Salvation (as Livia Bourne)

Anthologies

Christmas at the Club

Out of Print Books

Psychology of Submission, Corbin's Bend Series

Life's Unexpected Gifts, Corbin's Bend Series

Melting Silver, Red Petticoat Series

Call Sign Thunder

Bite Me – Vampire Anthology

Just Breathe – Anthology

Royally Mine – Anthology

Heroes to Obey – Anthology

A Lovely Meal – RWA Anthology

I Have Lived & I Have Loved - Charity Anthology

Dirty Daddies: 2021 Anniversary Anthology

THANK YOU FROM LIVIA

Like most authors, I love to hear from my readers. The art of writing can be a lonely activity at times. Authors sit alone, pouring our hearts into our stories, hoping readers will connect with our words and fall in love with our characters. It's easy to get discouraged at times.

And that's where you come in.

I'd sure appreciate it if you'd take a few minutes to drop me a line or better yet, leave a review to let me know what you thought of the book you just finished. Reader feedback, good and bad, is what helps me continue to grow stronger as an author.

Happy reading!

Livia

Manufactured by Amazon.ca
Bolton, ON

24619592R00097